Maybe h[...]
one kiss

Mitch leaned close enough to breathe in the scent that had teased his senses all day. Tessa smelled like exotic flowers and it aroused the hell out of him.

He just needed one taste. Just to see if she was as sweet as he remembered.

"There are so many potential customers here." Her voice faltered as he hovered near. "So many opportunities." She edged away as if that would discourage him.

Fat chance. He could tell by the agitated flick of her tongue over her lips that she wanted the kiss as badly as he did.

He skimmed his hand over her thighs. "I'm only interested in following up on one particular opportunity, Tessa." Sliding one arm around her waist, he pulled her to him. Her breathing hitched at the contact.

When her eyes drifted shut, Mitch homed in on her mouth for the kiss he'd dreamed about since their last one. Every drop of blood in his veins surged south. At just one blasted kiss.

What made him think he could ever stop at just a kiss?

Dear Reader,

The wintry Adirondack Mountains have never seen
such a heat wave as when Tessa O'Neal reunites with
former snowboarder Mitch Ryder...and ends up igniting
a relationship that's too hot to handle!

Marketing maven Tessa has as much competitive spirit
as the next woman. When her best friend challenges
her to stay out of her old flame's bed for a whole
week, however, Tessa begins to think some bets are
meant to be lost!

I hope you enjoy this steamy trip to the winter
wonderland of Lake Placid, New York, as much as
Tessa does. Visit me at www.JoanneRock.com to learn
more about my future releases or to let me know what
you think of this book. I'd love to hear from you!

Happy reading!

Joanne Rock

Books by Joanne Rock

HARLEQUIN TEMPTATION
863—LEARNING CURVES

HARLEQUIN BLAZE
26—SILK, LACE & VIDEOTAPE
48—IN HOT PURSUIT
54—WILD AND WILLING

TALL, DARK AND DARING
Joanne Rock

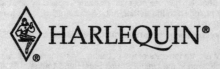

HARLEQUIN®

TORONTO • NEW YORK • LONDON
AMSTERDAM • PARIS • SYDNEY • HAMBURG
STOCKHOLM • ATHENS • TOKYO • MILAN • MADRID
PRAGUE • WARSAW • BUDAPEST • AUCKLAND

To K. Sue Morgan,
friend and mentor extraordinaire. Thank you for caring
about my characters as much as I do!
To the Rocks, for accepting me into their big, happy
clan and inspiring my love of the North Country.
And to Dean, a thrill seeker in his own right.

ISBN 0-373-69097-5

TALL, DARK AND DARING

Copyright © 2002 by Joanne Rock.

Visit us at www.eHarlequin.com

Printed in U.S.A.

____Prologue____

"WHAT WILL IT BE, Tessa? Truth or dare?"

Tessa O'Neal tossed back another Jell-O shot, the South Beach sunset twinkling rainbows through her thick crimson drink. How could she live in this paradise full of gorgeous men and still end up playing adolescent games with her girlfriend on a Friday night?

"Truth," she answered, loud enough for Ines to hear over the salsa music and happy hour crowd at the open-air bar on Ocean Drive. Forget the dare. Ines would think of something really embarrassing for her to do.

Ines Cordova's armful of silver bracelets jangled as she waggled a chiding finger at Tessa. Ines was more than Tessa's boss at Westwood Marketing. The two of them had been friends since Tessa was a freshman in college and Ines had been a grad student.

"That is your third truth in row, *chica*. I remember a time when you did not always run from a dare."

Tessa started to shake her head, then stopped when the thrum in her temples informed her she'd almost reached her Jell-O shot quota. "Let's not go there."

Tessa wouldn't be sitting around getting toasted if she hadn't had a colossally bad day. She'd planned this night out with Ines weeks ago as sort of a last hurrah before Tessa left Westwood to start her own business.

But the night had taken a decidedly glum turn since Tessa ended up breaking off her engagement to a perfectly great guy. What had she been thinking to give him his ring back just because he didn't leave her breathless every time he walked in a room like a certain guy she'd dated so many years ago?

She definitely didn't need to go there.

Where was the waiter with those shots?

"Now is the ideal time to go there." Ines shoved the plate of nachos they were sharing in Tessa's direction. "You say you do not know why you broke things off with Rob, but you do. The man is as much fun as a surfboard in Kansas, *querida*, and he is all wrong for you."

"He's reliable, and responsible, and he's a grownup." Unlike others she'd dated, especially one playful hunk she wouldn't forget even with a truckload of Jell-O shots.

Ines shook her head. Her long earrings hopped back and forth over her bare shoulders. "You need a man with a sense of adventure to match your own."

Tessa leaned across the table, hoping to make her point. "I've outgrown my sense of adventure, Ines. Maybe racking up one divorce and one broken engagement in five years has sapped it all. But I don't have any desire to dance on the table with a rose between my teeth or start a bunny-hop chain through the bar. It's not me." She pulled off the cheesiest nacho on the plate and crunched a big bite.

Ines scowled. "It was not the bunny hop, it was the locomotion, Tessa, and everyone had a blast."

Mouth full, Tessa shrugged.

"So you'll take a truth over a dare?" Ines asked, crossing her braceleted arms.

"Any day." She'd much rather reveal some inane secret of her past than sing a chorus of "It's Raining Men" on the strip.

Ines smiled. "Remember, you *have* to tell the truth."

Tessa sighed. "I hope you don't expect me to cross my heart and stick a needle in my eye and all that."

"I trust you. You still want to take the truth?"

"Sometime today. Yes." Tessa stared at her empty ring finger where Rob's engagement diamond had rested just this morning.

"Are you still in love with Mitch Ryder?"

The name blasted away all thoughts of Rob and his ring.

Mitch Ryder. The first man she'd ever been with. The man she couldn't help but compare all others to.

The wretch who'd ditched her to travel the world with a snowboarding team.

Her foggy brain realized she was taking too long to answer. "What kind of question is that?"

"It's the kind I want an answer to," Ines replied as she waved away their waiter.

"I can't answer that," Tessa returned, indignant on her own behalf. "That was eight years ago!" She waved the waiter back and ordered another round. She refused to make this a night of sappy regrets.

Ines leaned across the table when their server left. "Then you have to take a double dare."

"Fine." She was too annoyed to care about the consequences of a double dare.

Of course, she most certainly was not still hung up on Mitch Ryder. She'd had one husband and one fiancé since then, so how could she be? The point was, she just didn't want to discuss Mitch with anyone.

Especially not with Ines, who could pry confessions from a priest if given half a chance.

Besides, Tessa knew she might harbor just a little affection for the guy—even if he had walked away from the hottest affair ever to scorch across the northeast.

"Are you sure you don't want to just answer the question?" Ines prodded.

The next round of drinks arrived, and Tessa raised her shot glass full of jiggling cherry alcohol in mock salute. "That chapter of my life is closed, and I'm not talking, so bring on the double dare, girlfriend. I'm ready."

Ines retrieved her purse from the floor and pulled out a manila file folder with the Westwood Marketing seal on one corner. "Then I'd like to reopen the book, so to speak." She passed the file to Tessa.

A business dare? It was unlike Ines to challenge her with something so mundane and something Tessa would actually enjoy. Tessa loved a good test of her marketing skills.

Curious, she opened the file and stared at the business name on the cover sheet.

Mogul Ryders Snowboards, proprietor Mitch Ryder.

"Meet your new client, Tessa. I'm sending you to the beautiful Adirondack Mountains of upstate New York for your last week on the job." Ines sipped her shot as calmly as if she'd just announced she'd decided to paint her bathroom. "I hear there's lots of snow on the ground."

"What?" Tessa's heart kicked up a rhythm so fast

her blood outpaced the salsa music. Ines expected her
to go back to the scene of her long-ago affair and work
with the man who'd turned her world upside down?
"That's not a double dare, Ines, that's blackmail!"

"You are right, that's not a double dare, *querida*.
That's just the first part."

"There's more?" The file folder fell closed in her
hand as Tessa waited for the other shoe to drop. She
suspected the bunny hop would have been a walk in
the park compared to whatever torture Ines had
cooked up.

"*Si*." Ines's self-satisfied grin revealed every tooth.
"I dare you to stay out of his bed for the whole week,
Tessa."

A week? Last time she hadn't been able to stay out
of his bed for three days. The man was a walking aphrodisiac.

And somehow, Tessa had the feeling she'd just
agreed to a lethal dose.

1

THE LAST TIME Tessa O'Neal had set foot in Lake Placid, New York, she'd been on a quest to lose her inhibitions. Now, as she strode through the Adirondack hotel eight years later, she was determined to win back every last one of them.

Shifting the bag of Florida oranges from her father's groves on her hip, Tessa signed her name at the front desk. She always brought a bag of fresh citrus for her clients, and she figured it would help if she pretended this was just another marketing job.

A job that pitted her against the biggest temptation of her life.

Unfortunately, the four-star Hearthside Inn had been the site of many erotic interludes with Mitch. He'd worked in the pro shop the year they'd met, just about the time his career on the slopes had really taken off. His supreme confidence, his never-say-die attitude, had made Tessa feel more alive than ever before.

"Welcome, Ms. O'Neal." The smiling desk attendant greeted her. The woman's cable knit sweater and turtleneck looked at home in the Adirondack lobby with its oversize stone fireplace and sturdy pine furniture. "Mr. Ryder asked me to page him when you arrived."

"He's here?" Tessa battled a wave of panic. She'd

known he was running his snowboard business from the hotel, but she hadn't thought he might be working on a Sunday. She definitely wasn't ready to see him yet.

"He's here most of the time during the winter months. Want me to ring him for you?" She reached for the phone.

Tessa almost leaped across the counter. "No!" She succeeded in laying her hand over top of the woman's fingers to prevent her from picking up the receiver. Tessa smiled apologetically and let go. "I mean, that's okay. Just tell me where his office is located so I'll know."

"His rooms are just down this corridor to the left." The clerk pointed.

Tessa thanked her and purposely walked in the other direction. Right now, as long as she knew Mitch was occupied in his office, she'd just check out the mountain view from the patio for nostalgia's sake.

And to see if the back deck still encased the huge hot tub where she and Mitch used to watch the snowfall and gaze at the stars. Not that she was thinking of Mitch, she assured herself, just the beauty of those starry nights and how it had felt to have snow fall on her nose while hot bubbles tickled the rest of her.

Or had that been Mitch's fingers?

She adjusted her sack of heavy oranges one more time as she clicked her way across the hardwood floors. Rounding the corner of the downstairs bar, Tessa heard laughter from the afternoon patrons. She thought she knew where she was going until sunshine from a wall of windows blinded her.

For a moment, Tessa paused to squint in the bright

light, disoriented. Where she'd expected to find a door to the deck, she discovered a new addition to the Hearthside. A massive sunroom enclosed the outdoor oasis she had remembered, encasing the former patio area in glass.

The huge, sunken hot tub rested indoors, its continuous gurgle creating a rumbling backdrop of white noise. Its steamy depths fogged up a strip of windowpanes, but above the opaque area of the glass, Tessa caught her first glimpse of skiers tearing down Mount Van Hoevenberg and the towering pines that dotted the slopes.

Her interest in the scenery outside lasted all of a second, however.

Just about the time it took for a familiar laugh to draw her attention to the hot tub and three bikini-clad snow bunnies vying for the attention of one very content-looking male who sprawled in the water like a pampered Poseidon.

And no wonder the mermaid trio romped around the tub for his amusement. Even some ten feet away, Tessa took a step back from the sheer impact of the man, and she'd been semi-prepared to face him again.

Mitch Ryder—her off-limits boss for the next six days.

His eyes were closed as if in heady abandon, but the rest of his face looked as if it could have been carved from an Adirondack mountainside. High cheekbones and a square jaw made him appear fiercely male, but he smiled too often for him to look truly dangerous. Dark hair lay in one slick wave over his head.

Only his face and shoulders were visible above the water, leaving her hungry for a better view.

She recalled once when she'd sat in this same hot tub with him. He'd been naked beneath the water. The idea sizzled over her, turning her as warm and liquid as the bubbling bath. She doubted he'd be cavorting around the Hearthside naked in the middle of the afternoon, but she found herself straining for a peek into the blue depths anyhow.

Oh, no.

What was she doing?

Eight years later, she acted as moonstruck as ever around Mitch. Maybe she could sneak away now and he'd never notice. She would tell herself it had been a good thing to get her first viewing out of the way so she wouldn't be so cow-eyed tomorrow when they officially met.

It was a great idea.

In fact, she loved the idea.

Too bad her damn high heels were glued to the floor.

Before she could unstick her feet to make her exit, he moved. In a flash of sluicing water and flexing muscle, Mitch hoisted himself up onto the ledge of the pool and took a seat.

Tessa covered the involuntary squeal that rose to her lips. Whether she'd turned into a giddy coed because she could now see more of him or because he'd opened his eyes and might see her, she couldn't say.

But she refused to let her hormones hold her hostage.

She made a fast turn on her heel before she could change her mind, forgetting all about the oranges. The netting sack swung wide and pulled loose from her arm.

She watched in slow-motion horror as her citrus bounced and hopped in a cheerful orange beeline for the hot tub.

Tessa stood motionless as the first piece of fruit splashed into the pool right beside a redheaded mermaid. Mitch's gaze swung toward the orange and then to the impromptu citrus parade.

And then to her.

She gulped. Maybe she gasped. She searched for words and air and a small scrap of dignity to confront him with, because she definitely *wasn't* going to stand here acting like one of his groupies.

Striding forward, she managed a confident step that would have made Ines proud. Too bad Mitch chose that moment to rise to his feet.

She couldn't have looked him in the eye if her career depended on it. Her gaze wandered a slow path upward from his long feet to his lightly furred calves. His muscular thighs to his...swimsuit. The rippled plane of his stomach to tightened male nipples.

A memory of tasting his flesh in that very spot prompted her to lick her lips.

"Mitch." She breathed the word, unable to find her voice now that she stared into familiar gray eyes that had long dominated her fantasies.

"Hello, Tessa." His voice raked over her senses like fingernails on a lover's back. "Welcome back."

The steam from the hot tub seemed to kick up a few sultry degrees. It took all of Tessa's restraint not to loosen the belt of her trench coat.

"I didn't expect you here until tomorrow," she remarked, wishing she hadn't allowed herself such a long survey of him. She'd already catalogued way too many enticements. "I thought you moved to Tahoe," she blurted, needing to fill the sexually charged air around them with something besides her heavy breathing.

He grinned as he bent to retrieve her fruit. "Been checking up on me?"

Heat climbed her cheeks. He still possessed that slow, sexy smile. The one that had made her heart do back flips and her mouth go dry.

"Hardly." She knelt beside him and carefully avoided any random hand brushing as they picked up her oranges and put them in the sack. "I read about your accident in the papers, and they mentioned you were moving back to the States to recover." She wouldn't mention she'd scanned several articles to glean that much information, or that she'd been panicked when she heard he'd taken a bad fall down some Alpine mountain. "Are you okay?"

Now that they'd finished gathering her oranges, she and Mitch both stood.

Tessa tried not to stare at the broad expanse of his glistening chest.

"I'm better now that you're here." He reached for a towel and slung it around his waist. "Shall we head over to my office to talk?"

She had no choice but to agree. If they were going to plow through a week's worth of business, she couldn't afford to avoid him. But the temptation of she and Mitch in a private place sounded very dangerous for her dare...and her peace of mind. "I'm ready when you are."

Closing her eyes to shut out visions of Mitch's tanned skin, she sent up a prayer for some major inhibitions.

MITCH THANKED GOD he'd found a towel when he had, or Tessa would have seen rapid evidence of just how much he still wanted her.

He hadn't expected her until tomorrow or he never would have let her catch him lazing in the hot tub with the latest batch of bubbleheaded college girls to descend on the hotel. He'd snuck in when the pool was empty to give his knee some much needed therapy time. Could he help it if the coed crowd cornered him?

Some timing for Tessa's arrival.

He took her elbow and propelled her forward through the bar before she had a chance to protest. He had to do something to break that provocative, lingering stare of hers—the one that turned him on as much as if she'd touched him.

Even now, electricity zinged from her body to his hand, no matter how slight his touch.

She pivoted on her heel, swinging the sack of oranges into his shin. "Sorry!" She flashed him an apologetic smile.

He relieved her of the bag before she hurt someone.

"Those are for you, anyway," she informed him as she handed over the fruit. "Sort of a hello from the Sunshine State."

The Sunshine State had already been more than generous to him today. "Thank you." He took a step forward, eager to retire to the privacy of his office.

Not that he minded traipsing around the Hearthside in swim trunks—it certainly wouldn't be the first time—but he wanted to go somewhere quiet to talk to her, stare at her, convince her to have dinner with him...

She didn't follow his lead. Her feet remain rooted to the hardwood floor. "Would you rather just wait to talk until tomorrow?"

He shook his head. "Now is a great time."

Those bright green eyes of hers took a quick voyage south. "Wouldn't you like to, um, dress?"

He bit back a grin and the urge to give her the extended tour. "Only if you find me a distraction."

She straightened, then charged down the hall ahead of him in a staccato of clicking heels. "Not in the least."

He didn't know how she knew where she was going, but Mitch walked behind her, enjoying the view.

He'd bet Mogul Ryders she still had a killer body under that monstrous trench coat. Trim little ankles peeked out from the long hem. The belt around her middle nipped a tiny waist. Her face was more interesting than pretty, with full lips and a slight crook in her freckled nose. But somehow it all worked. She was the hottest thing Mitch had laid eyes on since she'd skipped out of his life nearly a decade ago.

He also happened to know she was a single woman, courtesy of her boss at Westwood. He'd been absurdly glad to learn that piece of information.

Not that he had any intention of claiming her forever. He wasn't any closer to being the stable kind of guy she wanted now than he had been eight years ago.

Still, he couldn't help but hope he could claim this next week.

She paused outside his door and stared at the brass nameplate. "They let you put the name on the door?"

He opened the door to usher her inside. "What do you mean *they*? I bought this place two years ago."

She gaped at him while he edged past her. "You own the Hearthside?"

"Long way up from pro-shop manager, huh?" He had to laugh. He still couldn't believe he'd wrangled this prime piece of real estate from its former owner. But he had, and this business belonged to him as much as Mogul Ryders.

"I'll say. Congratulations." A new light glimmered in her green eyes. Respect. "I never would have taken you for the type of person who would spend enough time in one place to run a hotel."

That single comment brought back a wealth of memories on why they hadn't stayed together. He flipped on his computer screen and avoided her gaze. "A management group takes charge when I travel."

"Oh." She apparently thought his globe-trotting ways were as irresponsible as ever.

He flicked on the gas fireplace to heat the rooms. The temperature had definitely dropped a couple of degrees since they'd walked in his office. He thought of other, more pleasurable ways to generate some warmth, but they had to talk business first. With more than a little regret, he reminded himself he needed her brains more than her body.

For now.

"Have a seat." He pulled a dry towel off the back of his desk chair and flung it on the seat so his suit didn't soak the upholstery. "I appreciate you coming up here, Tessa. When I started searching for marketing help, I wasn't expecting to find you. You've sure made your mark."

Tessa had told him eight years ago that she wouldn't travel with him because she wanted to do just that. Make her mark. He wondered if she was happy now that she'd achieved her goal.

She folded her coat carefully around her and took a seat across from him. "I travel a lot for my job. The trip wasn't a problem."

"I mean because of our history." He wasn't willing to act as if nothing had happened between them. She'd affected him too much for that.

Her eyes widened just a little, but she maintained her cool. "I assumed it wouldn't be an issue."

"Great. How about we get together for dinner later and we'll go over Mogul Ryders' business plan?"

She opened her mouth, but no words issued forth. On the second try, she managed, "Tonight?"

"The sooner the better, don't you think?"

"I haven't finished the marketing plan yet, though. Maybe if we wait—"

"Are we going to be able to work together on this, Tessa?" He eyed her with a level gaze, all thoughts of their past put aside for the moment. Sure he owed Ines Cordova big time for convincing Tessa to come to Lake Placid again—he hadn't been able to get Tessa out of his head ever since his accident. But no matter what he hoped might transpire between him and Tessa on a personal level this week, he wouldn't risk a misstep with the marketing.

"Of course we are. Didn't you specifically request my help in getting your new product line off the ground?" She returned his gaze, and for a minute, Mitch spied the steely determination that had no doubt helped catapult her to the top of her field.

"I've heard you're the best." He leaned closer. "But if you're going to find it difficult to work with me, maybe we shouldn't go through with this."

"It's been eight years, Mitch." She folded her arms across breasts he remembered all too well. "I think I'm over you."

He couldn't help but smile. "Good. Then you won't mind having dinner with me tonight. How is seven o'clock?"

She puffed out a small sigh and smoothed her hand over a stray lock of blond hair. His hand itched to mess it up again.

"Seven is fine," she said finally. "I just want to give you fair warning. I barely had time to repack my suitcase this weekend, let alone do thorough research. I really had intended on working alone tonight."

Perhaps he frowned at that, because she waved her hands in an impatient gesture.

"I don't mean to suggest this puts me behind on your account. You have my personal assurance that we'll come up with just the right marketing strategy for Mogul Ryders."

Mitch stood. "Okay. You want to take the nickel tour before I walk you upstairs?"

He pulled one of the hotel's robes off the back of the bathroom door and tossed it around his shoulders. Since his half-dressed state hadn't made her swoon in appreciation yet, he figured he might as well try another tack.

"I've kept my own findings and market research in here." He opened the door to a second sitting area and wondered if she'd notice the room's central furnishing. "Just help yourself to anything you might need."

He gestured to the stacks of brochures and folders on the file cabinets, but Tessa barely gave them a glance. Her eyes were glued to their old make-out couch in the corner.

Her breath caught.

Her cheeks grew pink.

She gulped visibly.

Maybe their weeks together had been as memorable for her as they had been for him.

Although the green love seat used to reside in the library, site of many of their out-of-control kisses, he'd moved the small couch in his office when he bought the ski lodge. Perhaps he wasn't really playing fair to tease her with it, but he couldn't resist the temptation to see her reaction.

She looked so much more buttoned-up than she used to. So off-limits.

When he'd first met her, Tessa had searched for adventure around every corner. She was the only girl he'd ever dated who gladly let him teach her how to snowboard. And she'd taken to it like a pro. He doubted she'd ever be so daring now. In her trench coat and navy pumps, she looked more fit for the boardroom than the slopes.

She faced him, cool as you please in spite of the steamy memories the love seat from the library *had* to call to mind. "Why don't you box up the files and send them to my room? In fact, I should probably settle in now so I can review my notes before tonight, Mitch. I really can compile a comprehensive plan for your company once I sit down and—"

"I know you can. That's why I hired you."

She arched a brow as if she didn't believe him.

"If you think I hired you because of what happened between us, you're wrong." Mostly. "I requested you because you're reputed to have one of the sharpest marketing minds on the Eastern seaboard."

That much was true. He'd been amazed to read her bio.

He stood in front of her, making sure to leave enough space between them to reinforce his claim that he only brought her here for business. He couldn't afford to scare her away. "I need an expert to help me make Mogul Ryders a blowout success."

Ever since Mitch had lost his ability to compete on the slopes, he'd hung his voracious need to succeed on his business. Tessa would be his ticket to realizing his goals.

She looked him in the eye. "I can do it."

He shook his head. He didn't want to hear the pat assurances she'd reel off to any of her clients. "But you said you hadn't fully researched my company. What if—"

"Frankly, Mitch, if you made snake oil, I could sell it for you with a kick-butt return on your investment."

He couldn't help a low whistle of admiration. The cool confidence in her gaze made him a believer. "Really?"

She grinned. "Really."

Mitch nodded, pleased his company rested in good hands and strangely proud to think Tessa O'Neal had turned into a business dynamo. "Then I guess I'll show you to your room and let you go to work."

He ushered her out of his office and toward the elevator. He didn't need to ask which room she was in.

He'd chosen it himself. Number 326, the executive suite.

She shuffled a few of the papers under her arm. "I'll have at least a portion of this mapped out by dinner. Shall we meet in the hotel restaurant?"

Mitch followed the progress of her stocking-clad ankles as she stepped on to the elevator. "How about we head over to MacRae's?" he suggested, dropping the name of their favorite restaurant as he punched number three.

Frowning, she cinched the belt around her coat a little tighter. "I don't know, Mitch. I—"

"They still fry up a mean lake trout." His mind conjured a wayward image of Tessa in her tan trench coat with nothing on underneath it but high heels. He really shouldn't torture himself like this.

"You should have gone into my field, Mitch," she muttered as the elevator doors swished open. "Which way?"

He pointed down the hall. "I'll take that as a yes?"

She didn't say anything as she paused in front of her door and slid the key into the lock. When the green light appeared, she pushed her way inside then turned to face him. She stood there a moment, poised in the entry, propping the door open with her hip. "Yes."

The word hit him with the force of a mogul at high speed—jolting his whole body and launching him through the air. God, but she packed a provocative punch.

She looked at him, her breathing a little fast, her cheeks tinged with color. Right then, Mitch knew he wasn't the only one who had mentally replayed every moment of their time together in the years since they'd seen each other.

He would have kissed her if he didn't think she might turn around and hop the first plane back to Miami.

But maybe she'd relax around him after they tied up their business.

"Meet you in the lobby around seven?"

She nodded. "I'll be there."

Backing away, he opted for a quick retreat before he did something stupid, like tug on the ties of that trench coat until it fell to her feet.

The door swung shut between them, but it didn't stop him from envisioning her every move behind it. Would she have that coat off yet?

Mitch hoped Tessa was every inch the marketing genius she was reputed to be, because the quicker they dispensed with the business portion of her trip, the faster he could get her back to that love seat in his office to relive a few fond memories.

2

HE'D KEPT the love seat.

No matter how much she tried to concentrate on developing a marketing plan, that one thought kept recurring in her brain.

Tessa paced the suite bedroom in her towel as she read over Mitch's file for the third time since her bubble bath.

Why had he moved the love seat into his offices? Didn't he remember what they had shared on that glorified pine bench? Or worse, what if he did?

Berating herself for her lack of focus, she planned her strictly business approach to tonight's meeting. She could do this. She had to.

If she could keep things professional between them for one week, she'd fulfill the dare and she'd be free and clear of Mitch, of Lake Placid, of her marketing job. She could start fresh with her sedate life next Monday, go online with her small clothing venture and forget this entire mishap.

Forget Mitch?

She tossed the file on the dresser and turned to the wrinkled clothing selections in her suitcase. Why had she ever agreed to spend the last week of her job in Lake Placid?

As she combed out her damp hair, Tessa noticed her watch read six-thirty. She had just enough time to rest her eyes before her appointment with Mitch at seven. She deserved a few minutes of downtime after her ten-hour trek to the Adirondacks and three-hour cramming session to develop Mitch's marketing plan. She'd been running on too little sleep all weekend.

Flinging aside her towel, Tessa slid between the taut sheets of the hotel bed and smiled. She snuggled into the embrace of flannel blankets and down pillows and tried not to think how much better her free time would be spent right now if she had a gorgeous man to massage her feet. A gorgeous man with gray eyes and the power to steal her breath.

Tessa squeezed her eyes closed more tightly, hoping to will away images of Mitch. Still, the tickle of cool sheets against her bare skin sent her mind on a vivid replay of this afternoon's meeting. Especially the first few minutes when he'd been soaking wet and half naked. All those hours on the slopes had given him a washboard stomach and thighs like iron.

If memory served—and she knew darn well it did— the rest of him was equally impressive.

Of course she shouldn't be visualizing her client in the buff. She wouldn't get involved with an adrenaline addict again, not when she'd promised herself she would embark on a new era in her life starting with her business venture next week.

She'd been so hung up on Mitch after she left Lake Placid the first time, she'd ended up married to a man eerily similar to him two years afterward. Her husband had seemed like a reserved man with a quiet banking job, but he'd sought his thrills in the stock market. He'd bankrupted himself, filched Tessa's credit card and run off with a wealthy figure skater before Tessa knew what hit her.

Too bad things hadn't worked out with fiancé number two. Rob had seemed so safe. So rooted.

So colorless compared to Mitch.

Yawning, she pulled the bedside clock radio on to her pillow and turned up the volume to prevent herself from sleeping. Why did she have to be attracted to such reckless men?

Oh, well. None of that mattered right now while she snuggled in the nest of blankets. She didn't have enough time to nap, and the dreamy love song on the radio defeated the purpose of music in her ear, so she spun the dial until she found a polka station and cranked the volume to full blast.

No way would she sleep now.

Or so she thought until she lost herself in sensual dreams. She could feel the heat of Mitch's hands upon her body, breathe the scent of his skin. They lay entwined on the old love seat in the library, their bodies a tangle of hungry limbs. The back of the love seat knocked a seductive rhythm against the wall.

Knock. Knock.

The sound transmuted, mingling with strains of Lawrence Welk.

"Tessa!" Mitch called her name. Too bad the hoarse cry sounded more like a shout of worry than one of ecstasy.

Knock. Knock.

"Tessa!" The object of her dreams shouted to her in time with an accordion riff blaring in her head.

She tried to blink her way out of her dream.

The door to her bedroom flew open. Mitch and a

middle-aged woman in a maid's uniform burst into her room.

"Are you all right?" Mitch's brow creased in worry. He seated himself beside her and gently shook her bare shoulder. He flipped off the accordion. "The room next door complained about the noise. Sorry about busting in here, but I got worried when you didn't answer the phone."

A shiver tripped through Tessa at his touch. Her dreams were still too close to the surface for her to hide her reaction to him.

The little maid peeked around Mitch, biting her lip. "She looks okay. Perhaps she was only tired."

"Thank God." His gaze pierced Tessa so deeply she feared he could read her recent wanton thoughts. She might have yanked the covers over her head to escape him if he hadn't turned away then.

"Sorry to have bothered you, Daniela." He nodded to the maid. "Tell your son we'll resume our practice schedule next week. Joey is really turning into a pro on his snowboard."

The woman beamed with maternal pride. "He looks up to you so much. Thank you for all you do for him."

Tessa blinked again as the maid left. She tried to gather her thoughts. "What time is it?"

He dropped down to sit on the edge of the bed and waved the clock radio in front of her nose. "It's quarter past seven. I was just starting to wonder if you were going to keep our appointment when I got a call about the noise up here."

Her sleepiness evaporated as the full impact of Mitch's presence in her bedroom hit home. He sat so close his thigh pressed against her waist and hip. In light of the awareness zinging through her, the goose down comforter separating them seemed as substantial as a bargain brand tissue.

She was definitely not dreaming.

"I guess I fell asleep." Too many cross-country trips for her clients. Too many Jell-O shots the other night. Only one more week and she'd reclaim her life.

He barely suppressed a laugh. "How could anyone fall asleep to the musical stylings of a German oom-pah band?"

She wriggled a few inches away from him in a vain attempt to halt the hormonal overload his thigh had instigated. The fact that she was naked beneath the sheets didn't help matters, either. If she had to stand much more of this, she'd be wrestling Mitch to the mattress in no time.

"Sorry I'm late." She tried to discreetly pull the covers closer to her chin. "If you give me five minutes, I'll meet you downstairs."

She hoped he would take the hint and go before she spontaneously combusted.

"Are you sure you're up to it?" He skimmed his hand over her forehead and leaned closer, a wolfish grin spreading over his face. "You feel kind of warm to me."

He didn't know the half of it.

Those long fingers called to mind the nights he had touched her, teased her in ways she hadn't experienced before or since.

Heat kicked through her even though she wasn't about to let herself be swayed. "I'm fine. I'll be in the lobby in no time."

She waited for him to leave, a prisoner of her nakedness under the covers.

He straightened but remained on the bed.

Mitch stilled his questing fingers, but his eyes were as predatory as ever. "Just out of curiosity, what have you got on under there?"

Every nerve ending leaped to life at his pretended interest, yet she would be damned if she would acknowledge it. Besides, she could handle his teasing. This was much easier than his caring.

"It's really none of your business." It strained her dignity to look coolly professional when she had a rat's nest for a hairdo and had no choice but to lie down.

"I notice your bathrobe is hanging on the back of the door." His voice turned husky and low as he jerked his thumb toward the length of navy blue terry cloth. "My guess is that it's a hell of a lot less than that."

Her skin tingled. Still, she pointed toward the exit. "I want you to go now."

"Do you really?"

No.

"Yes." She forced a determination into her voice she definitely didn't feel.

"If we were playing our old truth or dare game right now, Tessa, I think I'd have to penalize you for fibbing." He trailed a finger along her bare shoulder and then skimmed the length of her arm.

The touch reverberated through her, tickling nerves all the way to her thighs.

Lava streamed through her veins at the memory of past penalties. Mitch had been so very inventive....

But as delicious as those memories might be, Tessa had a job to do. She would never get it done by drooling over a man whose idea of commitment was to hire a management staff for his hotel property while he hopped the globe and broke hearts.

"I'm not here to play games this time, Mitch."

The quiet seriousness in her voice seemed to call him from his teasing flirtation.

He scrubbed his hand over his forehead and nodded. "You're right."

She realized how unfulfilling being right could be when she experienced a rush of aching loss as he backed away from the bed.

He held up his hands in mock surrender. "No games this time."

"No games." Clutching the sheet more tightly to her, she assured herself that's what she wanted.

Mitch had nearly reached the door when he paused at the dresser to examine a sheaf of papers she'd left there. "Can I take your Mogul Ryders file to occupy myself until you come downstairs?"

He scooped up her papers and began leafing through them.

"Could you wait with that? I'll only be five minutes."

Engrossed in the file, he barely acknowledged her. "See you then," he mumbled, folder in hand. He shuffled to the door as he read, seemingly oblivious to Tessa's protest that her notes were still too rough for his review.

At last the outer door finally closed.

Frustrated he'd absconded with her work, but very

happy to have escaped the temptation of his presence, Tessa breathed a sigh of relief.

That was close.

Much *too* close.

How was she ever going to stay out of Mitch's bed when she'd found herself naked with him inside their first twenty-four hours together?

She headed to her suitcase to choose her most conservative suit for their business dinner. After the close encounter in her bed, she needed a no-nonsense armor to ward off any stray charm he might fling her way.

Because no matter how appealing Mitch might be, Tessa had no intention of failing in her dare. She'd conquered the bunny hop, by God. She could darn well keep her hands off an overgrown playboy for one week.

MITCH WATCHED Tessa storm into the lobby about fifteen minutes after he left her room. He'd had just enough time to read over the file she had told him not to touch.

He could tell by the gray tweed suit and the all-business French twist of her hair that she was mad. The stern set to her jaw and the pursed lips reinforced the impression. But he could not compel himself to regret filching her file on Mogul Ryders. The marketing plan she'd sketched out for his enterprise was ingenious.

He handed over the sheaf of papers as a peace offering. "You're brilliant."

"You're a thief." She snatched it out of his hand and tucked it under one arm.

So much for charming her. "Sorry, Tessa. You

hadn't even closed the folder. Once it caught my attention, I could hardly put it down."

"You shouldn't have been in my room to start with," she grumbled.

He would bet she had no idea how the damp hair curling in sexy waves around her neck defeated the rest of her uptight hairdo.

"I suppose you would have been happier if I'd let you go deaf? C'mon, Tessa." He nodded toward the front doors, eager to pick that sharp brain of hers. "Let's have some trout and start this evening all over again. You can wow me with your plans."

Thankfully, she seemed to forget her annoyance once they got outside. Tessa was like a kid in the snow. She held out her hand to catch the snowflakes and tilted her nose in the air to let them fall on her cheeks. She even forgave him enough to take his arm as they crossed the slippery parking lot. She'd traded in her heels for black leather boots that hugged her calves.

He tried not to think about the legs inside the leather. He needed to focus on learning everything he could from her about promoting his company. This venture embodied all his hopes for the future. He couldn't afford to foul up another career since his professional snowboarding days had run amok.

She seemed more relaxed while discussing business over dinner, although Mitch questioned his wisdom at bringing her for a walk down memory lane at MacRae's. The café had an outdoor service window that accessed the ice pond. He and Tessa had once skated up for cocoa before heading back to his place....

And he really shouldn't think about that now. He

grilled her about marketing in an effort to distract himself. When he was thoroughly satisfied she knew exactly how to handle his account, he paid the check and ushered her outside.

"It's no wonder you're at the top of your field, Tessa," he remarked as they stepped into the crisp night air. "I can't believe you put all those plans together in a few hours."

Another inch of snow had fallen in the time they'd eaten dinner. Mitch knew he shouldn't court temptation by keeping company with her any longer, but she eyed the frozen pond and the skaters with open longing. He could empathize. Lake Placid in the winter seemed like a Christmas card come to life.

He nodded toward the bench near MacRae's skate-through window. "Want to watch?"

Shades of the adventurous Tessa flashed in her wide grin. "Sure. Cocoa's on me."

As she paid for the steaming beverages, strains from the restaurant's lone guitar player drifted through the skate-up window to serenade them.

"Don't be too impressed with my work, by the way," she remarked as they seated themselves on the rough-hewn plank that served for a bench.

He blew on his cocoa and watched the steam curl into dancing white wisps in the cold air. "You're being modest."

She shook her head. "Hardly. I had the office fax me a lot of the contact names and the links for the Web site we'll make for you." She shrugged, as if compiling fifty pages worth of resources had been no big deal. "We'll hit your target audience with an interactive, flashy site. Between that and the other ideas, we'll get a broad range of exposure."

He believed her. And felt relieved for the first time in months. He'd been so worried about taking his company to a new level that he hadn't been able to really relax in ages. But somehow Tessa's conviction rubbed off on him. With her by his side, he could make his new venture a success. It had been easy to buy the Hearthside, which had been a well-run business to start. The self-sufficient hotel would never give him the same degree of satisfaction as getting his snowboard business off the ground.

"So why did you leave Tahoe?" she asked between delicate sips of hot chocolate.

He stared at the tiny rim of foam on her top lip. Eight years ago he could have leaned over and licked it off. He wondered what she would do if he tried it now. "Too young. Too full of X Games wannabes."

She licked her lip, sending shockwaves of primal hunger right through him.

"You mean too many youthful Mitch Ryders."

The guitar player inside launched into "Bad Moon Rising." Mitch knew half the kids in Tahoe would think Credence Clearwater Revival was an environmental movement. "I was never *that* young."

Tessa snorted.

"I take it you disagree?"

"You used to be pretty wild."

The key words being used to be, Mitch thought with disgust. Since his accident, he hadn't even hit the top of Whiteface. He still spent some time showing the local kids the tricks and twists that had once put him at the top of his game, but he'd never have the edge that he used to. Fortunately, he had a new game to conquer, a new field to dominate. The business world.

And as long as he had Tessa to help him, he would be on top in no time.

He groaned at the image. On top.

He definitely didn't need to think about how much Tessa liked being on top.

Tessa watched Mitch stare at the stars and wondered what he was thinking. He didn't seem to want to talk about the past, but Tessa didn't want to leave their winter wonderland just yet.

While she was thinking of a way to linger, a boy broke free from the skating pack and careened toward them.

"Look out!" he shouted, his face contorting into a theatrical version of fear.

"Hey, Joey," Mitch called. "No pratfalls over my guest."

Seconds before slamming into their bench, the boy regained control, gliding to a stop beside Mitch.

"Pretty good, huh?" The kid tried to play it cool, but he looked at Mitch with undisguised hero worship in his eyes.

Garbed in the garish colors the snowboard crowd favored, the boy looked to be somewhere between eight and ten years old.

Mitch ruffled the boy's hair. "Did your mother tell you I'm busy this week with business?"

Joey grinned. "That's okay, I think I've got all the moves down."

"Yeah, right. Stay out of trouble this week and I'll take you to Whiteface next week when I have some time."

"Really?" The boy's cool facade vanished, and his voice was pitched a notch higher.

"Really. Now take yourself off so I can get some work done." Mitch gave the kid a nudge and sent him cruising backward on his skates.

Tessa watched the exchange with interest, curious about the ties Mitch seemed to have to the community. He'd been more of a wanderer when she'd first met him.

"That's Daniela's son," he explained. A smile played about his mouth. "You remember, the maid who was with me when I came into your room when you were, um..."

He touched her shoulder and skimmed his fingers down the length of her arm, a vivid reminder of the caress he'd given her earlier when only a blanket had separated her naked body from him.

Tessa straightened, prepared to curtail any flirting before it started. "He seems very nice." She searched for a new conversational route before Mitch could look at her with that teasing light in his eyes again. "So where are you living now? At the hotel?"

He had dropped the subject of Tahoe and his accident so fast she hadn't figured out where he called home at the moment.

"I got a good deal on a log cabin a mile up the road from the inn."

"You bought it?"

"You sound surprised."

She shrugged. "I can't picture you settling down in one place."

"I'm grounded for awhile."

His grimace made it clear he found the idea of staying put as painful as the monstrous fall that stalled his former career two years ago.

"It's been a long time since I read the article about your accident, Mitch." She'd practically memorized it, actually. Yet she wanted to hear his version. "What happened?"

"Stupidity."

She wouldn't press. She watched a family of skaters clutch one another as they giggled and wobbled their way around the pond. The crisp scratch and skritch of the blades on ice reminded Tessa of the home-wrecking figure skater her husband ran off with. But sitting here under a snow-speckled velvet sky with Mitch, the thought didn't rankle as much as it had in the past.

"I caught a lot of pop coming off the pipe," Mitch finally explained.

She made the time-out sign with her hands. "I don't know if I can interpret snowboard-ese anymore."

"I had too much height over one of the banks at a Swiss meet." He gestured with his hands, using his cocoa for the bank and his free hand for the snowboard. The snowboard hand sailed above the foam cup. "I should have limited my moves to something simple so I could have regained control, but I had been on fire all day."

Tessa remembered all too well what Mitch was like when he was on fire. On the slopes, it had meant he owned the course.

In her bed, it had meant she'd be smiling for days.

"Let me guess. You used the height to do something outrageous and reckless."

"I got spinning so fast." He maneuvered the snowboard hand into a single snowboard finger and demonstrated it twirling around and around in the rising steam from the cup. "Observers say I spun well over a thousand degrees. Guys frequently spin nine hundreds or ten-twenties, but this was beyond that."

Tessa cringed. How could he be proud of an accident that nearly killed him? "And you lost control?"

He frowned and stared at his pantomimed performance as if he didn't know where to move the players next. "More like I lost concentration for a fraction of a second. I think I let myself enjoy the moment for an instant, and in that nanosecond, I miscalculated the landing."

He allowed the finger snowboarder to fall over and careen downward past the cocoa cup to land in a heap on the wooden bench. "I didn't just hit the pipe and fall, I flew butt over boot heels halfway down the mountain." He shook his head as his gaze turned from the drama of his fingers and locked on her. "I lost control."

The regret she discerned in his eyes almost made her want to throw her carefully constructed professional persona to the wind and reach out to him.

But she refused to dare anything more with this man.

She had another dare she planned to honor, and it involved thinking with her head instead of her heart.

"I'm sorry, Mitch." Too late, she realized her voice conveyed all the emotions she had sought to suppress. The throaty whisper reverberated in the silence like the echo of a far-off church bell.

Embarrassed by her transparent feelings, she stared

downward, only to spy his hand laying on the bench beside her thigh. Almost touching.

He yanked it back after a moment and drained his cocoa. "It was a good lesson," Mitch declared, crinkling the cup and tossing it into a nearby trash can with a hook shot. "I'm more cautious now. I have a business of my own and employees to consider. I can't afford to be reckless anymore."

Tessa chose her words with care. "You've invested a lot of yourself into Mogul Ryders." He might be creating some stability with his business. Yet she'd be willing to bet if given a snowboard or skis—or a meaningful relationship, for that matter—he'd be as impulsive as ever.

"It means everything to me, Tessa." He leaned forward with his elbows on his knees, eyeing the action on the ice like a benchwarmer eager to get in the game. "That's why I'm so glad you're going to help me get the new product line off the ground. You've got the expertise I need."

"Westwood Marketing has a great team. They'll make sure your line makes an impressive debut." She knew her first pang of regret about leaving her firm next week. A part of her would have liked to supervise the implementation of her plans for Mitch's company.

"Your firm has quite a reputation. But it's you I trust." He winked.

A warning buzzer went off in Tessa's head. She had to make certain he understood that she wouldn't be part of the package after Friday. "Of course, my contribution is complete once your plan is polished and approved."

Mitch straightened. The music from inside MacRae's stopped, and the dinner crowd applauded. "What do you mean?"

Silence surrounded them but for the scrape of blades on the ice and the far-off giggles of the skaters. The falling snow insulated them from the rest of the world.

"I'm leaving my firm. Setting up the marketing plan for Mogul Ryders is my last project."

Mitch's jaw flexed in silent testament to his vexation. "Why? They don't pay you enough? Because I can hire you—"

"No." She didn't care to hear how much he needed her brains when he'd never had any need for her heart. "It's not that. It's the pace. I don't want to spend all my free time in airports anymore."

He clasped her shoulders in his hands. Logically, she knew his skin must be cold from their time outdoors. His touch sent heat waves through her anyhow.

"But this is big, Tessa. This is my whole life."

He'd said much the same thing to her eight years ago when he asked her to trot the globe with him while he chased his dreams on the pro circuit. She hadn't been able to make him happy then, either.

"I'm sorry, Mitch. I've already given my notice."

"How much longer will I have you?"

She knew he didn't mean the question in the provocative way her ears heard it. That didn't stop the shiver that tripped through her in response.

She took a deep breath and told herself she only had

a few days to endure the sensual torment of just being in the same room with him. She could do this.

Braving his gaze, she repeated the motivational mantra she had been using to fulfill Ines's dare. "I leave in just one week."

3

MITCH STARED into her green eyes, willing her to change her mind. Yet he could tell by the mutinous thrust of her chin he wouldn't be any more successful at a Vulcan Mind Meld now than he had been the last time they'd parted.

As he walked her to his truck, however, it occurred to him that he had infinitely more life experience than the last time she'd left him. And he had more than his heart to forfeit this go-round. The job security of everyone in his company rested on whether or not he could get his snowboard line off the ground.

That meant he'd have to commit himself to making Tessa stay. If she was quitting the job because she worked too hard, maybe he could woo her into helping him by showing her a good time. When was the last time Ms. Trench Coat and Heels had some fun?

With only one week to change her mind, Mitch knew he couldn't afford his slower approach anymore. As of now, he was a man on a mission.

TESSA OPENED a reluctant eye and scanned her hotel suite for the source of the incessant pounding that woke her before her alarm sounded. She abhorred the thought of leaving her nighttime cocoon of flannel sheets and down comforter. She also couldn't go back to sleep until the knocking ceased.

"Tessa?" Mitch's gravelly baritone drove through her door. "You awake?"

She groaned a reply, hoping her incoherence would be enough to send him away. She'd have a hard time living up to the dare if she had to confront such a sexy voice first thing in the morning.

"There's at least a foot of new snow from last night," he called. "You should see it."

Like a child rooting for a snow day, Tessa brightened at the weather report. She shimmied partway out of the covers. "Did they clear the pond yet?"

"Nope. It's pristine. Untouched. You can be the first snow angel out there if you hurry."

A little tremor of excitement skittered over her, but she couldn't be sure if it had to do with eagerness to get outside or a desire to see Mitch again. What would it hurt to have a little fun? And they wouldn't be anywhere near a bed....

She tossed off the remaining blankets and slid to the floor. "Ten minutes, tops. I'll meet you out front."

"I think you'll want to let me in," Mitch persisted.

"Not a chance. Unless you have coffee?" She dashed around the room, flicking on lights, pressing the button for a gas flame in the fireplace, running a comb through her hair.

"Among other things."

Curious, she jabbed her toothbrush around her mouth then opened the door a crack. "Like what?"

Mitch thrust forward a room service box with two powdered doughnuts and steaming cups of coffee. "Breakfast."

She opened the door wider to admit him. She ignored the starchy voice of her conscience that balked at entertaining a client in her hotel room. This was Mitch, after all. It seemed dishonest to pretend they'd never meant anything to each other when they had spent two weeks of their lives practically glued together.

The mental picture accompanying that thought sent a sensual wave of heat through her thighs and belly.

She hoped her cheeks weren't as flushed as they felt. "Great! I'm starved."

Wandering inside, he set his offering on a polished pine coffee table.

How could he look so good first thing in the morning? Her gaze drank in his lazy stride, his easy smile. He wore a long wool coat with a red scarf trailing the collar—a far more conservative look than the trademark neon apparel he used to wear in his snowboarder days. His one concession to his former fashion sense was a tiny troll with neon yellow hair pinned to his lapel.

She looked away when she noticed he was observing her as candidly as she had been regarding him.

He cleared his throat. "You look very nice in red, by the way."

Had he meant to comment on the blush she felt on her cheeks or the flannel pajamas she'd bought in the gift shop?

"These are the most comfortable clothes I've ever worn." She dropped onto the sofa and pulled a corduroy pillow onto her lap. The tasseled blue bolster seemed a pitifully inadequate barrier between her and walking animal magnetism.

"But they're not very practical for making snow angels."

She grabbed a doughnut. "I'll come up with something suitable. Have a seat." She motioned toward the wing chair. The one farthest away from her corner of the couch.

He remained standing, one arm behind his back. "Like what? The trench coat?"

Tessa frowned, wondering what he was hiding. "What have you got back there?"

The sound of crinkling paper greeted her ears as he jiggled whatever he concealed. It sounded like a paper bag.

"Something suitable." He tossed a bag with the pro shop logo on her lap and sat down.

"Mitch, I can't—"

"It's nothing." He took the lid off her coffee and handed her the cup. "The owner always gets the best deals."

She took a sip of coffee, telling herself she shouldn't open the bag. But she knew it contained clothes of some sort. She had a damnable weakness for clothes. "I really shouldn't."

Mitch bit into his doughnut, sprinkling white powder down his sweater and groaning at the presence of vanilla cream in the center.

"Actually, this is a necessity. If you're going to familiarize yourself with my product, you'll need protective gear." He handed her a pastry. "It would be unprofessional of you not to accept."

"Unprofessional?"

"Definitely."

How could she refuse? "You really missed your calling, Mitch. Your selling skills would knock mine off the chart." Laughing, Tessa set the doughnut aside and tore into the bag. "Snow pants!"

"Ski pants."

She admired the trim black spandex and thanked God his company made snowboards instead of surfboards. Ski pants would be much kinder to her legs than a French bikini high-rise. "Is there a difference?"

"Aerodynamics. You can pick a jacket to go with them on our way out. I wavered between green or red."

"Is a jacket considered protective gear also?"

"Absolutely."

She had to laugh, surprised at their easy rapport in spite of the undeniable chemistry between them. Had he been this considerate when they'd been together eight years ago? Certainly, he'd always been this much fun.

Perhaps this week's trip would help her remember not to take life so seriously all the time.

Or was that a dangerous line of thought?

She tossed off the pillow shield and stood. She would face Mitch's charm head-on. "I guess I'd better get dressed if we want to see the snow before the rest of Lake Placid wakes up."

Mitch frowned, but he rose, too. "I've got a lot of things I want to show you today." He strode toward the door.

A whole day with Mitch. No pillow armor to protect herself from his blatant appeal. No conservative business suit to remind herself to act in a circumspect, professional manner. How would she keep her distance from him if they kept having fun?

She spied the answer stacked on top of her brief-case. "I'll bring my notes. We'll get lots of work done."

He shook his head. "Don't bother. You'll never cap-ture the right mood for the marketing pieces if you in-sist on approaching everything as work. Mogul Ry-ders is about having fun."

She nodded, accustomed to listening to her clients' directives. There was just one problem with this par-ticular command.

She knew from personal experience that having fun with Mitch might be more temptation than her over-loaded senses could handle.

MITCH COULDN'T HELP but notice Tessa's entrance at-tracted more head turns than a tennis match when she sashayed into the lobby.

Damn, she looked good. How was it she could gar-ner more attention in a ski suit than most women did in a swimsuit?

Or maybe it was more a matter of her neon yellow coat dazzling everyone in a fifty-yard radius.

He eyed her selection, surprised she hadn't gone for her usual conservative palette. "I take it they were all out of navy blue?"

The sound of her throaty laughter sent a shot of heat through him.

"I had a red one in my hands, but this one just called to me. Loudly."

"You look great."

It was a simple enough remark, yet it hung in the air between them, laden with more meaning than he'd meant to give it. Tessa stared at him for a long mo-ment before tucking a blond strand behind her ear.

"Thank you."

Reminding himself to go slow with her, he sought to break the tension by fingering the tiny pin on his black jacket. "You need a troll to match."

"I'm going to let that remain your unique fashion statement. This coat was enough of a change for me today." She grinned, her eyes alight with mischief he hadn't seen in too many years.

Which might mean Phase One of his Make Tessa Stay plan had been a success thus far.

His rationale had been simple. If Tessa wanted to quit her job because she resented spending her free time in airports, maybe she would accept a position with him if she saw she could have fun while working.

Lucky for him, he had an inside angle on what she liked to do for fun. He'd felt a twinge of guilt this morning when he'd bribed his way into her room with breakfast. But with Mogul Ryders's future on the line, he couldn't afford to fight fair.

He needed her by his side.

He wanted her in his bed.

MITCH WAS prepared to push the envelope when they returned to the inn after a day packed with every winter sport imaginable. He hadn't made concrete headway with her yet, but one potential weapon remained in his persuasive arsenal.

The love seat.

They stamped snow off their boots and hung their jackets on the massive coat rack at the front door.

"You'll never get me to go down the luge run again," Tessa announced, padding her way toward his office suite in thermal socks.

They had agreed to wrap up some business before they ended their day. Mitch couldn't help but hope their meeting yielded more than just a marketing plan.

He led her to a different door than the one she'd been in before—the door that led to their love seat.

He let her enter first.

"Give it up, Tessa. You adored it." Mitch couldn't help but admire the sway of her hips as she walked.

The ski pants she'd worn all day accentuated every curvy nuance, taunting him with the memory of the sexy body her staid business suits couldn't quite hide.

"Sure I did." She hesitated a moment when she noticed the small couch, but she sank down into the soft green cushions anyway. "That's why I screamed the entire time, right?"

"That's how I know you loved it." He switched on the fireplace in front of them and dropped down on the love seat a few feet away.

Her cheeks flushed before she turned to stare into the blaze. The shrieking she'd done today hadn't been exactly like the primal cries he remembered from their days spent together between the sheets, but the sound had still fired his blood.

She ignored his remark and seemed to make an effort to keep their conversation on track. "The bobsled was awesome."

"Best bobsled run I've ever been down." He closed his eyes to savor the memory. Seated behind her on the sled, he'd practically had his legs wrapped around her for an electrifying sixty-three and half seconds.

Now she propped those legs on a leather hassock, and Mitch's mouth watered.

"Have you ever thought about doing a regional

publicity tour to promote your snowboards to the locals?'' she asked suddenly, as if the business wheels had started turning in her much-too-busy mind again.

He shifted beside her, partly to get closer to her, partly to ease the arousal that had plagued him ever since they'd sat down. ''I'm not thinking about work right now, Tessa.''

In fact, his thoughts had more to do with wrestling those ski pants from her thighs, but he knew he'd be a fool to move too fast. He should be grateful she'd spent all day with him, ostensibly reviewing possible future product lines for Mogul Ryders by trying out every winter sport Lake Placid had to offer.

He wouldn't push her, damn it.

But maybe he could allow himself one kiss.

He leaned close enough to breathe in the scent that had teased his senses all day. She smelled like exotic flowers. The scent was definitely more neon yellow than navy blue, and it aroused the hell out of him.

He just needed one taste. Just to see if she was as sweet as he remembered.

''There are so many potential customers here.'' Her voice faltered as he hovered near. ''So many good opportunities.'' She yanked a corner of the throw blanket over her lap, as if the frail network of yarn would discourage him.

Fat chance. He could tell by the agitated flick of her tongue over her lips that she wanted the kiss as badly as he did.

He brushed the afghan away, skimming his hand over her thighs. ''I'm only interested in following up on one particular opportunity, Tessa.''

Sliding one arm around her waist, he pulled her to

him. Her breathing hitched at the contact of his fingers underneath the hem of her sweater. He paused, drinking in the feel of her smooth skin as he splayed his hand over her back.

When her eyes drifted shut, as if she surrendered all control to him, Mitch homed in on her mouth for the kiss he'd dreamed about for eight years.

He groaned at the absolute perfection of her. The lips that were soft as a bubble bath. The scent that drugged him into behaving like a hormone-overloaded teenager. The taste that wavered between earthy-sexy and divinely sweet.

Every drop of blood in his veins surged south. At just one blasted kiss.

What made him think he could ever stop at just a kiss? He left her lips long enough to sample her neck and the hollow valley at her throat. Her fingers bore into his shoulders, and a strangled cry reached his ears.

"Mitch." She gasped in time with the hungry swipes of his mouth over her neck. "We can't."

He could think of about a million reasons they definitely should. The first being her heart hammering against his chest at least as fiercely as his own.

"Why not?"

She inched backward, inserting a sliver of space between them. "Because this will interfere with our work. Besides, we've been down this path, and it doesn't have a happy ending."

Her words rained ice on his wayward libido. Not nearly enough to freeze it over, but enough to resurrect his ability to reason. He sure as hell couldn't jeopardize his plan to make her stay because of his hunger for Tessa.

If she left in a huff because he couldn't keep his hands off her, then his business suffered. More than anything, he needed to please her first.

Himself second.

In that case, he needed to take it slowly...maybe get away from the temptation of the inn and the sensual memories it posed, or he'd be right back to trying to kiss her within twenty-four hours. He wanted her so much he couldn't see straight.

Then the perfect solution hit.

He slid away from her. "How about that publicity tour?"

She blinked. "What?"

He was gratified to see the pulse still throb in the small valley between her collarbones. It must have been at least a little bit of a struggle for her to pull away, too.

"Spending time together around here seems destined to get us into trouble." They'd whiled away too many hours necking on this very love seat. "Let's hit the road and do that promotional thing you mentioned. What do we need, a couple of days?"

He shifted away from her to help keep a leash on his hunger for her. Maybe the extra days on the road would buy him the time he needed to convince her to stay.

He would indulge his seduction scheme later, *after* he'd persuaded her to stick around.

She nodded. "At least." She rose from the small couch and backed away from him with the caution of a rabbit facing a tiger. "But what about the other things we need to get done? The marketing plan—"

"We'll plow through the rest of the plan when we get back." He needed to get out of here before he did something that would make her run, something like stroke his hands over that fantastic body of hers. "Get together a list of places to hit, and we'll get underway first thing in the morning."

"Good idea—focusing on our work to keep our hands off each other." She mustered a lopsided smile before retreating to the elevators. "'Night, Mitch."

His body still thrummed with thwarted desire, but he'd made the right decision. No way would he scare off Tessa before he'd had a chance to revisit their sizzling past.

He stood, smiling at the efficient way he had bought himself some time alone with her. He would convince her to stay in the marketing business at the same time he worked on his seduction scheme. As long as he moved slowly with her, everything would be fine.

Of course, he'd have his work cut out for him trying to take it slowly when they were alone in the enforced intimacy of his truck cab.

Just him and Tessa and a cramped bench seat.

For three days.

Suddenly the idea of taking it slow sounded like pure torture. Their little love seat packed full of memories didn't seem nearly as dangerous as the sexually frustrating hell on wheels he had just consigned himself to for the next three days.

4

FROM THE BAY WINDOW of the executive suite, Tessa looked down on the parking lot. She watched Mitch load his truck with the help of a blond-haired man sheathed in an electric green ski suit.

She'd met the younger man when she had toured the hotel to network with the staff last night. Shawn Dougall managed the pro shop when he wasn't competing on his snowboard. Shawn's hunger for the next thrill, his passion for the sport, reminded her of the Mitch she'd met eight years ago.

He helped Mitch secure various sizes of Mogul Ryders snowboards to a customized rack in the truck bed while an audience of Gore-Tex–clad snow bunnies admired their efforts from ten feet away.

Tessa observed the scene, already accustomed to the appreciative glances Mitch garnered from females of all ages. Something about the daredevil mentality attracted women in hordes.

Of course, Tessa told herself, she wasn't one of those admirers. At least not anymore.

She couldn't believe Mitch wanted to leave the Hearthside to spend three days on the road.

Together.

As soon as she had agreed to it, she'd known it was a world-class dumb idea. How could she resist him when he'd be no more than two seat belts away?

But Mitch had seized the idea like a lifeline after their kiss. Maybe he'd felt as shaken by the spontaneous combustion incident as she had, because he suddenly seemed eager to resurrect some professional boundaries in their relationship.

Definitely a good idea, no matter what her wayward fantasies might suggest to the contrary.

She cradled her cell phone against her ear, stalling in the hotel room because she wasn't ready to face Mitch yet. Instead, she'd called Ines.

"So is he as gorgeous as I remember?" Ines Cordova's Latin accent purred through the handset. Ines had accompanied Tessa and two other girls on that long-ago trip to the Adirondacks. She had witnessed Tessa's heartbreak firsthand.

"Times two." Tessa sighed as she surveyed Mitch stride to the pro shop for another board. His gait was no longer as purposeful as it used to be. He still bore the marks of the snowboard accident that had nearly killed him.

That slight swagger in his walk didn't come close to diminishing the brash charisma of the man, however. Apparently the snow bunny throng drooling over him didn't think so, either.

"And, saint that you are, you have no inclination to seduce him?"

"Of course not." Tessa turned her back on the tempting window view, crossing her fingers to ward off any negative karma that fib might cost her. "I came here to fulfill a dare and prove I was finally over him. Don't you think seduction would defeat the purpose?"

"Maybe, *chica*. But don't let your pride rob you of a chance to make things right with him this time."

"I am making things right this time." Tessa tossed a lipstick in her purse, then gathered notes for the trip. "If I had done things right eight years ago, I would have never wound up in Mitch Ryder's bed."

In the background, Tessa could hear her friend's computer keys clicking and her jewelry clinking. From her jeweled toe rings to her designer hairpins, Ines was the most decorated woman Tessa knew.

"Please do not tell me you are going to forsake the best sex of your life this time because of a ridiculous dare."

"You're the one who dared me!"

Ines snorted. "Tessa, the Jell-O shots have surely worn off enough by now where you must realize I dared you so you'd feel more compelled to take Mitch's job."

"No." Maybe. "As the matter of fact, I didn't realize that. Did Mitch put you up to this?"

"He asked me to try my best to get you to Lake Placid," Ines admitted. "But the dare was all my idea."

"That's cold and calculating manipulation, Ines." Not that Tessa could be mad at her best friend if she tried. No doubt Ines had some twisted romantic notion that Mitch had changed over the last eight years.

"I just don't want to see you make another mistake, *cara*. If you try to marry a lifeless banker type again, I'm not keeping my mouth shut."

"Gee, thanks." Tessa slid into her trench coat, being careful not to jar the phone from its niche on her shoulder. "I know how hard it is for you to speak your mind."

She moved toward the bay window, unable to resist one last peek.

"I only want to help." Computer keys and bracelets quieted on the other end of the phone. "I thought you should have run off with him the first time around."

Tessa stilled.

It would have never worked, would it? They'd been too young to know what they wanted.

"It's ancient history between us." Tessa watched Mitch talk to a group of passing skiers and hoped her words were true. "Did you receive my e-mail with our itinerary for the next few days?"

Papers shuffled one thousand miles away. "Saranac Lake, Tupper Lake, Ticonderoga…not exactly major metropolitan areas. Why bother?"

We can't keep our hands off each other in this town. "We'll get hometown support and word-of-mouth sales."

The soft tapping of Ines's computer keys was renewed. "Do what you want, *chica.* But remember you aren't in Lake Placid merely to work. It wouldn't hurt to mend fences."

As if he felt Tessa's gaze upon him, Mitch turned from his worshipful audience and looked unerringly into her third-floor window.

Flustered, she gave him a halfhearted wave. "I thought I was here to stay out of Mitch's bed."

By the way her blood heated at the sight of him, it seemed she might fail miserably.

"Forget the dare!" Bracelets jangled a discordant note. "If anything, ending up in bed with a man who genuinely lights your fire might be the best thing for you after the Rob debacle. You ought to heal the past before you start a new life and a new business."

Tessa backed away from the window. "Thanks, Oprah. But that's your agenda. Not mine." She squeezed the bridge of her nose in an effort to staunch the tension headache that always followed this sort of discussion.

"You'll never be happy until you resolve your feelings for him." Despite all her flash and sophistication, Ines seemed to enjoy her role of mother hen even though only six years separated them.

"Then you'll be pleased to know I've got things resolved. I'll be back in my office on Sunday to clean out my desk." Tessa fanned herself with a file folder.

"Try to at least give yourself a chance—"

"Whoops! Look at the time." Tessa couldn't bear this discussion. Not now. Not when she was about to launch into three days of nonstop Mitch. "If you need me, I'll be at this number." She pushed the end button and shut off her phone.

If only she could turn off her hunger for Mitch so easily.

She'd accepted Ines's dare to prove she could resist the Ryder charm and move on with her life. No matter that Ines had only used the dare to manipulate Tessa into close quarters with her former flame. She was still going to uphold her end of the bargain.

Mitch would just have to remain in her past where he belonged.

MITCH KNEW he was done for as soon as he spied the trench coat and high heels. This would be the longest three days of his life.

Tessa marched across the parking lot, amazingly steady on her three-inch shoes now that the snowplow had cleared a path. A tousled topknot of blond hair bounced in time to her step. She wheeled a small overnight bag with one hand and toted a bulging briefcase with the other.

He allowed himself a long moment to enjoy the view before giving himself a pep talk. Keep things professional for the good of Mogul Ryders. "Lose your boots?"

Green eyes blinked at him. Her face looked scrubbed clean but for a slash of peach lipstick. He experienced an outrageous craving for fruit. Why hadn't he packed one of the oranges she'd brought him?

"No. I just prefer to wear shoes for business meetings."

"We're touring the north country, not Madison Avenue, you know. How about your ski jacket?"

She shoved her suitcase toward him and frowned. "It's in my hotel room, not that it is any of your affair."

Affair.

His body responded instantly to her choice of words. He closed his eyes to shut out a steamy vision of Tessa beneath him. "Right. Definitely not my affair."

He packed the suitcase into the narrow space behind the front seat and held the door for her.

Her step up into the cab parted the trench coat, treating him to a view of stocking-clad calves and a hint of thigh.

Pure torture.

He slammed the door shut with more force than he'd intended, but she didn't seem to notice. Inside the truck, Tessa dug into her briefcase and extracted a file.

Mitch said a quick prayer for restraint, then hopped in on the driver's side. "Where to first?"

She squinted at a map tucked in the leather binder on her lap. "Saranac Lake doesn't look too far from here. We'll hit the newspaper to drop off a press kit and the sporting goods store to show off the new boards."

"You know this might take more time than you're accustomed to." He hoped Tessa's big city ways wouldn't turn off the locals. The people who made a living in the Adirondacks were a breed of their own. "People around here might like to shoot the breeze a little."

She didn't look offended. In fact she smiled. "I'm in public relations, Mitch. I think I'll manage."

He pulled on to Route 86 and left the Hearthside Inn in his rearview mirror. Just as he'd feared, his attraction to Tessa didn't fade in the distance along with it.

Damn. He would work overtime this trip to keep seduction on the back burner and his mind focused on his business and making Tessa stay.

The thought sobered him. Miles of snow-covered pines passed him in a blur as he recalled his father's lifelong dire predictions of his failure. No matter how many trophies Mitch accumulated or how big a purse his snowboarding career earned, his father had always harbored faith his overindulged last born would screw up eventually.

And he had.

In a split second of bad judgment, Mitch had

watched his career spiral downhill along with his body.

For the last year, Mitch had worked without pause to secure a comeback success—through business if not on the slopes. Now all he needed was Tessa by his side to take his venture to the next level.

And prove his worth.

If he wanted her to stay and help him, he had to walk a fine line between his plan to show her a good time and his desire to show her an earth-shattering time.

"I think you turn here, Mitch." Tessa's voice broke through his reverie.

He barely controlled the truck as they took a slippery turn down a main street. Cursing his preoccupation, he downshifted and reminded himself Tessa's safety was a hell of a lot more important than Mogul Ryders.

Frowning, she straightened in her seat and turned on him. "I hope your quest for an adrenaline rush doesn't carry over to the driver's seat. It's not too late for me to hitchhike."

Mitch had never seen her this angry before. She was usually so low key. Controlled.

"Sorry, Tessa. I don't think we were that close to death."

She studied him a long moment before nodding. "Maybe not."

He chanced a quick glance in her direction. "I might risk me, but I'd never risk you."

She gave him a halfhearted smile. One that said she didn't quite believe him. "It wasn't really your fault." She tucked a folder into her briefcase. "My ex-husband drove like a maniac in a quest for the thrills he couldn't get through his job."

"Ex-husband?" Mitch choked the word out over the lump of jealousy congealing in his throat.

She made a dismissive gesture with her hand. "We've been divorced nearly three years. We were all wrong for each other." She pointed toward the left side of the street. "I think that's the newspaper building."

Mitch focused on his U-turn to keep himself from saying something stupid. "You were married?"

Of course, he'd never had much luck preventing himself from doing stupid things.

"For three years."

He did the math in his head as he parallel parked. "You got married two years after you left Lake Placid?" Two years didn't hurt so bad as one year would have. Still, her admission had sucker punched him.

"Have you been married?" She asked him as calmly as if they were discussing his target audience.

"When I get married, I'll stay married." He clicked off the truck ignition.

"You'd stay married, would you?" Fiery red color lit her cheeks. Her full lips compressed into a thin, flat line. She looked ready to spit nails.

"Damn straight, I would." His parents had stuck it out, no matter what. Sure they disagreed, but they didn't drink, didn't cheat and they didn't beat each other. The stability of his old man's marriage was one of the few things he really admired about his dad.

"Well, good luck staying married to a man who runs off with an internationally renowned skater who has family in every eastern European country." Tessa wrenched at the door handle, but her hand slipped. "You try finding your spouse in Croatia, Mitch. I guarantee you, even you and your high and mighty ideals would have a hard time!"

Succeeding in operating the handle, she slid to the ground and yanked her briefcase behind her.

Damn.

He hadn't even been able to stay on neutral ground with her for half an hour. Even worse, Mitch couldn't help but think he'd provoked her out of jealousy.

If sparks were already flying thirty minutes after leaving Lake Placid, how the hell was he going to survive the week?

TESSA ENJOYED the satisfying slam of the door and stomped up the sidewalk. She marched right past the newspaper office and left Mitch behind. She had no intention of screwing up his professional reputation or her own by talking to anyone from the press while she was upset.

Mad as she was at herself for letting him get to her, she couldn't let his comments pass unchallenged. She understood his commitment to marriage. But he shouldn't have played Mr. Know-it-all about a situation he couldn't possibly understand.

"Tessa!"

Her step slowed. Much as she tried, it seemed she couldn't storm away from him forever.

He caught up to her in no time in his sensible hiking boots. "Wait a minute." He grabbed her by the wrist. "Please."

The please got to her. Between the gentle tone of his

voice and the heat of his palm through the leather of her gloves, she had no choice but to hear him out.

"I have no right to judge you." The pressure around her wrist increased ever so slightly. His thumb slipped onto a patch of her skin above the leather.

"No right at all," she agreed. The slight touch over her pulse coaxed her heart to a faster rhythm.

For a moment, she couldn't help but wonder how she could have married anyone else knowing Mitch Ryder still walked the earth and that he affected her this way.

Why hadn't she realized it before?

She'd been a fool not to resolve her feelings for him long ago. Because she hadn't, she'd only been able to give half of herself to her husband. To her fiancé. To any man she'd dated for the past eight years.

A small group of children bundled in hats and boots walked by them on the street. Mitch pulled her into an alleyway between buildings.

"Is he the reason you never came back?"

Gray eyes pinned her, backed her into the solid brick wall behind her. He couldn't have surprised her more if he had announced a desire to become a CPA.

"No!" Her pulse thrummed a jumpy dance. She fought the urge to lift a hand to his chest. "Why would I have ever come back after what happened between us?"

His last step brought him flush against her. Her briefcase teetered on the tips of her fingers and fell to the ground.

"Because of this." He didn't have to spell it out for her—she felt the *this* straining against her belly. "Because we spent the most incredible two weeks of our lives together."

"I..." She struggled to find the voice that seemed to have deserted her. "What was there to come back for, after the way we parted?"

"Remember naked Marco Polo?"

She closed her eyes to ward off the memories of their sexy games in the hot tub.

He planted his hands on the wall behind her, bracketing her between his arms. "Or how about the erotic rounds of truth or dare?"

His breath fanned her cheek.

Tessa swallowed, speechless.

"Or do you need a reminder?"

Desire sped through her like a narcotic, drugging her senses and weighing down her limbs. A reminder would kill her. "No."

Too bad she wanted one more than she wanted her next breath of air.

He touched an errant strand of hair that blew across her cheek and made a clumsy attempt to tuck it into the knot on her head. "You ever let your hair down anymore, Tessa?"

She took a deep breath, both grateful and a little disappointed he hadn't kissed her. "Not very often." She summoned a smile in a vain attempt to lighten the moment. "I find it only gets me into trouble."

"I'll take that as a hint." He eased away from her slowly, as if it pained him as much as it did her.

A chilly breeze ruffled the air between them. Tessa welcomed its cooling effect.

"I think we'd regret treading down that path again, don't you?" Her heart wished he would argue with her. Her head knew he wouldn't. But then, Mitch had thrown her ability to think clearly into an uproar ever since she'd watched him haul himself out of the hot tub.

Bottom line, Mitch would trade Mogul Ryders and his personal life in a nanosecond for a chance to hit the international circuit again, wouldn't he? The man would never give up his thrills for the sake of settling down.

"I think we'd love every minute of it, honey." The corner of his mouth lifted in a rueful attempt at a grin. "But I know you'd leave again, and that I *would* regret."

Her words from eight years ago drifted back to her. "My life isn't about a perpetual quest for fun. Sooner or later, I'd need roots to go home to. Roots you don't seem to have an interest in growing."

He nodded, accepting her statement as truth even as she longed for him to contest it.

"I know. And I will do everything in my power to respect that, Tessa." He retrieved her briefcase and folded the handle into her palm. "Do me a favor?"

Tessa nodded, mute with frustration and unfulfilled yearning for something Mitch could never give her.

"If you decide to ditch the hairpins again, will you let me know?"

THEIR CONVERSATION in the alley replayed in Mitch's head as he watched her charm the socks off yet another crusty Adirondack newspaperman.

Everywhere they went today, Tessa had worked marketing magic. The Saranac Lake paper took a photo of Mitch with his new snowboard line and promised to run it alongside a file photo of him on the slopes for a Sunday feature piece.

At the sporting goods stores, Tessa delivered sales materials and persuaded the managers to step outside and look at the boards firsthand. She never left anywhere without making a friend, and the majority of time she got them invited for a cup of coffee.

Mitch stirred cream into his fourth cup that day and listened to her compare farming notes with a well-known north country columnist. Even in her trench coat and designer heels, she looked more at home here than he did.

Of course, that's why she wouldn't get involved with him again. Tessa wanted to put down roots, to have neighbors over for tea.

And no matter how much her peach-colored lipstick drove him crazy, no matter how much the trench coat made him long to undress her, Mitch knew they wouldn't work together long term.

He still harbored dreams of international fame. Or at least enough recognition to prove he wasn't the failure his father predicted he'd be.

He didn't have anything more to offer her than he did eight years ago. In fact, he probably had less because now he could never compete professionally again. Except for the Hearthside, his worth started and ended with Mogul Ryders, a business that hadn't fully gotten off the ground.

That didn't stop him from wanting her anyway.

5

SHE HAD TO STOP wanting him.

Tessa sat in the truck, eyeing Mitch's every move as he strode out the door of the second roadside hotel they'd stopped at this evening.

Never had she seen a man look so good in a pair of jeans. And she'd been around the world at least twice according to her Frequent Flyer miles.

Hadn't she come to Lake Placid with the idea that she would exorcise her fascination with Mitch and move forward in her life? So why couldn't she keep her eyes off him?

He bounded down the steps and gave her the thumbs up. Thank goodness. The first inn they'd stopped at had only one room left. They'd lit out of there as if the hounds of hell nipped their heels.

Mitch leaned into the truck and pulled his overnight bag from behind the driver's seat. "Two rooms, two bathrooms, and the owner makes breakfast in the morning."

From the way he sprinted around the truck and re-moved her bag, too, Tessa guessed Mitch felt as eager as she was for a little time apart. The intimacy of his pickup only fueled the chemistry that sparked be-tween them.

"Why don't we turn in early?" Mitch helped her out

of the cab. "I'll work on a more concrete itinerary for tomorrow so we can book hotel rooms in advance."

She shook her head. "I need you to review the mock-ups for Mogul Ryders's updated Web site design."

There was no way around it. If they were going to work together, they needed to spend time together. Tessa couldn't afford to let him off the hook tonight.

He flashed her a sheepish grin and opened the door to the bed-and-breakfast. "You're going to eighty-six my homemade site?"

She followed him up the stairs. He obviously knew where they were going.

"You created it?" She was impressed. "It has nice visual appeal. And it's a feat of engineering that a homemade site hasn't crashed with the traffic you're already getting."

Pointing her into a small bedroom wallpapered with ivy and orchids, Mitch dropped her bag on the floor. "Really?"

"Really. A lot of amateurs who build their own sites crash within a few months if they get too many hits. You must have read up on it."

For a moment, international hotshot Mitch Ryder looked tongue-tied in the face of her small praise. He finally shrugged as if the hours of study he must have undertaken were no big deal. "Thanks."

But she must have misinterpreted his expression. He was well accustomed to the spotlight and all the accolades that went along with it. The thought that he would be so flattered by a compliment from her was absurd.

"You're down the hall?" She stuck her head around the door frame to orient herself.

"I've got ivy and daffodils." He grimaced.

She tweaked the pin on his lapel and winked. "It'll match your doll's hair."

"For your information, this is not a doll. It's an icon."

"Ah. I see." She stepped into her room. "How about you and your doll come over in about twenty minutes for some tea and we'll go over the Web sites?"

"You're pushing it, Tessa." He jabbed a warning finger in her direction, but his grin looked anything but threatening.

She tried to envision he-man Mitch surrounded by orchids and sipping tea. Unfortunately, her imagination didn't paint him any less gorgeous. In her mind's eye, she imagined him flinging his teacup aside in a fit of passion. They'd roll around on her bed amidst file folders and paper.

She fanned herself with a manila envelope. Damn. Why did she have to possess such a vivid imagination?

HE WOULD HAVE picked better surroundings for their meeting than the floral purple nightmare, but once again, Tessa overwhelmed him with how much she had accomplished in just a few days.

Westwood's suggested designs for a Web site lay scattered around him on her bed. Stacks of research for potential links weighted the nightstand. A cup of tea, which he studiously ignored, perched atop the papers.

"When did you find the time to do all this?"

"I didn't. My company puts this stuff together and sends it to me so I look impressive."

He shook his head, not buying her story completely. "You must have given them some direction." He fingered a graphic of himself snowboarding. It seemed like another man now. The athlete in the picture looked invincible, spinning in the air on his board.

"I talk on the phone a lot after hours to get things done." She eyed the artwork critically, as if trying to decide which design she liked best. "Westwood is a very virtual company. I tell someone what I want and then access it on my computer a few hours later. It's amazing."

She'd abandoned the suit jacket she'd worn all day and paced the room in wool trousers and a rose-colored blouse. The upswept hair and strand of pearls still screamed *professional*.

She paused to sip from her cup of tea. He did his best not to leer as her lips parted to take a drink. He remembered much too clearly how her mouth felt on him.

The purple walls seemed to close in, shrinking the space to nothing but him, Tessa and the bed.

What had possessed him to take her on the road for a promotional tour? At least at the Hearthside Inn they could have conducted the meetings in the dining room, the lobby, the elevator...anywhere but in a room with a bed.

He searched for something—anything—to reroute his wayward thoughts. "Why leave a job you're so good at?"

She replaced her cup on its saucer and took a seat opposite the bed. "I'm tired of the travel. The past two years have been a blur of weekends in airports and weeknights spent prepping for client meetings. I love my job, but I want more out of life than work."

Mitch settled against the headboard and hoisted his feet onto the bed to listen. "Why not just take a marketing director position for a small business? Your travel would be minimized and you could—"

"I can't."

He shook his head. "I'm not saying you'd have to come work for me. You could—"

"I can't." She folded her arms and tilted her nose in the air. "Did it ever occur to you I might already have my next step in life mapped out?"

He rubbed a hand over his chest, feeling the impact of her words like a blow. Of course she'd have her life mapped out. Tessa O'Neal always had a plan.

That meant she wouldn't be coming to work for Mogul Ryders anytime soon.

"I guess it should have. I've just been too caught up in wondering how to make you stay."

Her gaze flew to his, her eyes wide and round. "Stay?"

"It's no secret I'd like you to stick around and help me grow the business, but if you already have plans—"

"I have plans." As if eager to end the discussion, she marched toward the bed, full of purpose.

Mitch wanted to ask her about those plans, but she didn't give him a chance.

"Do you have a favorite among these graphic designs?" She shuffled through the artwork with smooth efficiency.

The fun-loving, luge-riding Tessa vanished, leaving business-dynamo Tessa in her place.

She checked her watch. "Because I'd like to get as much of the new site firmed up as possible. I have an appointment in ten minutes."

Mitch dropped his feet to the floor. "You have an appointment?"

"Yes."

"Here?"

"In ten minutes. Could we go over the designs one more time?" She reached for the photo of him in an aerial spin riding a lightning bolt instead of a snowboard. "How about this?"

He tossed the photo on the bed. "Who the hell are you meeting at a bed-and-breakfast in Ticonderoga at nine o'clock at night?" He would kill whoever it was. Tessa might light out of his life come Sunday, but she was his until then.

The rumble of an engine sounded outside. Headlights flashed through the thin curtains at the window.

Tessa smiled. "Why don't you see for yourself?"

He sure as hell would. What made her think she could have a rendezvous with someone else while he was footing the bill for her hotel?

Following her down the stairs to the owner's living room that doubled as a lobby, Mitch ground his teeth. It might be torture to be stuck in a bedroom with an irresistible woman he could never have again, but it was a torture he wouldn't give up without a fight.

Boots tromped up the plank steps outside. Tessa moved toward the door to open it, but Mitch stepped in front of her before her hand touched the knob.

"Allow me." He flung the door open wide.

And was greeted by a toothpaste-commercial smile and a thousand watts of lime green spandex.

"Hey, Mitch!" Shawn Dougall, manager of the Hearthside Inn's pro shop and one of Mitch's former snowboard buddies, stepped inside the great room. "The lady boss told me to bring these over."

He pulled in a dolly with two crates and proceeded to unload them on the floor.

Tessa shoved Mitch aside and passed a check to the newcomer. "Thanks, Shawn. Sorry to drag you out here so late."

He took the check and winked. "For you, Tessa, no problem."

"You had him come all the way out here because you forgot these?" Mitch nudged one of the crates with his foot, wondering when Tessa had found time to woo his staff right under his nose.

"They didn't arrive at the inn until late this morning." She bent over one of the crates and went to work on the wire latch. "But I had to have them to give away while we're on the road."

At last the fastening sprung loose, and she pulled open the wooden case.

"Oranges?" Shawn sounded disappointed.

Tessa ripped into a drawstring bag. "Try one."

She offered him a bite, a challenge in her eyes. She looked like a subtropical Eve handing the fruit to a lime-green Adam.

This Adam was equally enthralled.

"Oh, God, this is good." Shawn tore into the citrus like a man who'd been living on fast food. "Wow."

Mitch leaned over the crates to examine the small bags. Each one bore a silver card with a snowboard and a lightning bolt on the front. On the back, a note proclaimed the gift courtesy of Mogul Ryders and Westwood Marketing. Their names and Web site addresses were included.

"I hope that's okay with you." Tessa watched him with a hesitant expression on her face. "I know we haven't committed to a logo for the company yet, but at least everyone will remember who they're from."

"It's fine." Of course, it was better than fine. Between Tessa's naturally gregarious manner and her thoughtful gift, Mogul Ryders would be remembered everywhere they went.

"My father's orange groves are also advertised inside each bag," she explained. "I get them at a reduced cost because I let him promote his business, too."

Shawn wiped his mouth on the back of his glove. "Geez, she's sharp." He gave Tessa the full-blown toothpaste smile and jerked a thumb toward Mitch. "You got anything going on with the old guy?"

Mitch draped a friendly arm across the younger man's shoulders with as much force as he dared. "She's got plenty going on with the old guy, Shawn. You'd better get back to the inn before you miss your curfew."

Shawn stood at the door, oblivious to how much he had disrupted Mitch's evening. "But I don't have a cur—"

Mitch helped him out the door with a shove.

"What about the qualifying rounds tomorrow? Do you think you'll be—"

He nudged harder, not wanting Tessa to hear about the competition. He wasn't ready to watch others excel in a sport he would never compete in again. "Good luck, Shawn. Thanks again."

He shut the door as Shawn shouted goodbye to Tessa.

"Now, where were we?" He turned back to find Tessa apologizing to the bed-and-breakfast owner for disrupting her living room.

After echoing her sentiments, Mitch took Tessa's arm and led her up the stairs to her room.

"We were trying to settle on the graphic look of your Web site," she reminded him. "But I'm curious about something else first."

He dropped onto the bed, causing her design work to bounce and shift on the orchid-covered spread. "What's that?"

"What's this about a qualifying round?"

Tessa could see the muscles in Mitch's jaw flex, and she knew she had asked the wrong question.

"It's nothing." His usual easy humor disappeared.

"If it has to do with snowboarding, it might be an ideal opportunity to start a buzz about your product line."

"It's not." He rifled through the scattered artwork and chose one of the few designs that didn't incorporate him into the graphic. The piece used stick-figure lines to portray a person flying over a mogul, crouched on a snowboard as if prepared for impact. "I like this one."

"Wouldn't you rather use one that cashes in on your fame and reputation?"

He flicked the design Frisbee style over the bed. "What reputation? As a washed-up old guy?"

"At thirty?"

"Snowboarding is youth-driven. I was probably peaking at about the time I met you."

"From what I can recall, it was quite a peak." In more ways than one.

His eyes slid over her with slow deliberation.

Tugging a chair to sit near him, she regretted her knee-jerk response and tried to look as innocent as possible.

"I got the best scores of my life at the meet the week I met you."

She felt her breath catch. She didn't know if she could take an evening of remember when with Mitch.

Their knees rested less than a foot apart. Tessa's gaze flicked over the softly worn denim of his jeans and imagined what it would feel like to smooth her hand over that length of faded indigo.

"You were the hometown hero," she managed, forcing herself to carry on a conversation as if she weren't imagining off-limits scenarios with the dynamic man beside her.

She thought back to the Mitch of the past. She'd dragged her girlfriends out of bed every day to watch him and then screamed herself hoarse cheering for him.

"It seemed like it," Mitch agreed. "Even if Lake Placid is a far cry from my hometown."

She'd forgotten that. Mitch had grown up in New York City. After a couple of years at the University of Vermont, he had started touring the U.S. snowboard circuit. His longest stint had been spent in Lake Placid.

"Do you get home much anymore?"

"My dad and I relate better long distance." Mitch sifted through the graphic designs and pulled out one of himself holding a trophy aloft. "He only wants to hear from me when I'm in winning mode."

Tessa felt a rush of appreciation for her mother and father. She was blessed to have the two most normal, supportive parents on earth. "He's fortunate, then, to have a celebrated athlete for a son."

Mitch laughed, the sound a harsh bark in the quiet room. "He feels pretty damn unlucky to have an up-start businessman for a son. He equates entrepreneur with shiftless swindler with no prospects."

"You know better than that." She caught herself before she put a reassuring hand on that denim-covered knee. Touching Mitch was a risky proposition, and she couldn't afford to close the distance she needed to maintain between them.

"Until I make a success of this thing, I'm inclined to agree with him."

"There are other ways to measure success than the bottom line."

"Sure there are. Like if you get the highest score, or the fastest run, or the biggest jump. But I can't com-pete for those things anymore. I'm just looking for a fat bottom line now."

"Along with your father's approval." The comment slipped out before she could censor herself.

Mitch stiffened.

"Sorry. That was uncalled for."

He held up a hand as if to halt her apology. "No. It's semiaccurate. I probably got into this venture to prove to my dad that I could still come out on top. But the more involved I got, the more it meant to me."

He looked over the graphic work again and sighed. "And at this point, if I want it to be a success, I should trust the expert. You decide which design would be best."

His faith flattered her.

Especially now that she understood how much Mogul Ryders meant to him.

She dug out the retouched photo of Mitch riding the lightning bolt. "This is my favorite."

He took the graphic and shook his head. Nostalgia lurked in his gaze. "No one will even know Mitch Ryder in another year or two. There are new kids to the sport who haven't even heard of me."

"Your snowboard line will cement your legend. They'll remember you now."

Frowning, he turned the picture this way and that. The gesture reminded her of the way he used to study a snowboard run, memorizing every angle.

"This doesn't even show the product."

Tessa moved to sit beside him. Looking over his shoulder, she felt all the more certain she'd chosen the perfect image. "It gives an idea what it is. Plus it makes you want to find out what it's about."

He stroked his jaw. His brow furrowed.

She knew unconvinced when she saw it. "Lightning draws on the ideas of speed and excitement, both inherent in the sport."

"I do sort of like Day-Glo orange for a lightning bolt." He turned that slow, teasing smile on her.

She hadn't realized how close she'd sat to him. Their proximity had seemed perfectly appropriate ten seconds ago as they talked business.

Now, as the air between them heated, it seemed downright decadent.

She scooted away. "Then I guess that's all settled."

With a broad sweep of her arm, she started gathering the art samples and clearing off the bed.

Mitch seized her hand, halting her hurried movements. "Honey, things are about as far from settled as they could possibly get."

His eyes assured her he wasn't talking about graphic design.

Heat flashed up her arm and refracted through the rest of her body. Desire she'd suppressed for so long— ever since she'd left Mitch—roared to life at his simple touch.

For the woman who made her living with words, the inability to speak took her by surprise. Her mouth moved, but no sound came forth.

He leaned closer. "Maybe we should try to get this thing settled between us instead of running away from it."

The cold chill of fear knifed through the liquid warmth in her limbs. She extracted her hand from his. "I'll keep my running shoes, thanks." Grabbing the remaining papers from the bed, she stood and backed away.

Mitch tracked her movements with his eyes, saying nothing.

Some of the hastily gathered papers slipped from her grasp. She squeezed them to her chest.

"I mean, things are settled for me."

He rose, his presence filling the room, rocking her well-ordered world. "Would you care to make that a truth or dare?"

"Truthfully, no."

His smile couldn't have been more triumphant if

he'd just taken first prize in a snowboard freestyle event.

"Come on, Tessa. I dare you." He stepped closer, his gaze locked with hers. "Play with me."

The sounds of her breathing, her overactive heartbeat, filled her ears. She wanted to answer the dare, damn it. Since when did she back down from a little challenge?

"Only if I get to go first." She must be crazy. "Truth or dare, Mitch?"

"Truth. Ask me anything."

He'd already managed to take her by surprise. Hadn't he always gone for the dare before?

"What are you thinking right now?" The words fled her lips before she could weigh them, another by-product of Mitch's proximity.

Muddled thinking. Impulsive speaking. The man had her so confused she didn't know what she was doing anymore.

With one finger, he traced the fall of her hair along the side of her face, eliciting chills down her spine and warmth through her limbs.

"I'm thinking about how much you used to like making love seated on my lap. You remember that, Tessa?"

Heat flooded her cheeks as sensual memories assaulted her in clear, living color. How could she forget the way he'd claimed her on their love seat? On the bench seat of the old truck he'd had back then? On the floor of the pro shop storeroom after hours?

Thankfully, he didn't seem to expect a response.

"I just keep wondering what you would do if I pulled you onto my thighs right over there on that bed." His fingers paused as they reached her shoulder, then continued to trace across her collarbone to the top of her breast.

"Would you be as wild as you were back then, Tessa? As reckless and—" he leaned close to whisper in her ear, his body causing her every nerve ending to leap in anticipation "—loud?"

Her eyes fell to half-mast for one dangerous moment. It was difficult enough to focus on work when she wanted Mitch so badly. But how could she ever focus on it again, knowing that his thoughts were every bit as graphic and hungry as her own?

The papers in her arms crinkled under the pressure of her restless, edgy arms, reminding her why she shouldn't allow Mitch to woo her back into his bed.

She shook her head, clutching her papers in weak defense. "You win this round, Mitch. I concede."

"Next time, I want us both to win."

"I can't let that happen." Her voice was less than a whisper, throaty and raw with unanswered need.

"If that's the way you want it..." He moved toward the door.

"That's the way it is." Her voice lacked conviction, but at least she was able to meet his gray gaze head-on.

"Good night, Tessa." His piercing stare saw right through her. "Pleasant dreams."

As the door shut and her paperwork slid to the floor, Tessa knew she'd see his face when she closed her eyes that night. And far from pleasant, she'd bet the farm that vivid dreams of Mitch would tease and torment.

No doubt, it was going to be a long night.

6

DAWN FILTERED through the blinds, sending a shaft of morning sunlight onto Mitch's right eye. Normally, he would have fallen right back to sleep. Knowing Tessa slept in the room next door, however, hadn't made for the most restful night. He awoke instantly, envisioning her tousled and rumpled two yards away.

He cursed plaster in general and his daffodil covered wall in particular.

Shoving aside the yellow curtains at the window just above his bed, he watched the snow fall outside. About an inch of new powder covered his truck.

Tessa would be happy. He remembered her saying once that growing up in the Sunshine State had made her appreciate snow. Funny how he remembered lots of things she'd told him, stories she'd shared, from their time together.

Tessa.

He'd promised himself he wouldn't hit on her and mess up the professional relationship they needed this week. But he'd broken that promise in a few days' time.

Maybe we should try to get this thing settled between us instead of running away from it.

The words had fallen from his lips without thought. But he wanted her so bad he couldn't see straight.

Leaving the Hearthside Inn had done little to thwart his desire for her.

And she hadn't exactly responded in kind to his idea of hot sex to solve their problems. She had looked ready to flee, clutching her papers in a death grip as she backed away from him.

What was so wrong with what he'd proposed? He'd kept his distance so far because he didn't want to compromise their business relationship and because he didn't need another killjoy telling him his days of thrill seeking on the slopes were over.

But what would it hurt if they spent a few nights together before she disappeared from his life again? Instinctively, he knew Tessa was too much of a professional to drop his account if their relationship didn't work out. She had too much pride in her work to pull a stunt like that.

Maybe he'd been looking at this situation all wrong. Instead of fighting the crazy attraction he still felt for Tessa, he ought to be finding a way to indulge it. Exploring the heat between them might ease the tension. Ignoring it sure as hell hadn't eased anything.

Especially not for him.

Full of new resolve, Mitch tossed the covers aside. He ran a hand over the rough texture of his jaw as he padded toward the bathroom.

A synthesized, electronic version of "Jingle Bells" resounded through the room, halting him.

His cell phone.

He rummaged through his bags to find the obnoxious phone his sister had sent him for a birthday present and pressed the talk button before the beeping second refrain could begin.

"Hello?"

"The course is wicked, man." Shawn Dougall's gravelly voice shouted through the receiver. "You should be here to see it."

In the background, Mitch could hear the sounds of a snowboard competition getting underway. Electric guitars wailed from someone's boom box. A scratchy public address system was being tested amidst a high-pitched whine. Athletes shouted morning greetings, no doubt interspersed with the occasional exchange of tales about how they'd spent their night on the town.

Two years ago, Mitch would have been among them.

"Business calls, Shawn. I've got a real job now."

"I thought snowboards *are* your business. Wouldn't the lady boss want to be here to see the qualifying rounds? It might, you know, help her do that advertising stuff."

Mitch leaned against the bathroom's pedestal sink and scrubbed a weary hand through his hair. The kid was right.

Tessa would be more than a little upset with him when she found out Mitch hadn't told her about the biggest snowboarding event so far this year. She might understand why he'd kept his distance, but she'd never understand why he hadn't given her an opportunity to attend as his promoter.

Of course, he hadn't been thinking about where Tessa's time would be best spent professionally. He'd been thinking about buying more time with her so he could finagle one more night in her bed.

"You're smarter than that neon kiwi ski suit lets on."

A long pause followed his statement.

"Meaning she'd want to be here, right?"

He fed Shawn the line he'd been telling himself the last twenty-four hours. "We aren't even ready to sell the boards yet. We don't have literature to give to vendors or a completed Web site to send them to. Our time is better spent up here."

Away from the competition. Away from the scene that would make Mitch hunger for the spotlight and a life he could never return to.

"Suit yourself. But people are already asking about you."

"Yeah?"

"Well, they're asking about the new boards mostly. But everybody's heard you're behind that gig. And Joey is going around telling everyone that doesn't know already," Shawn said, referring to the Hearthside maid's son Mitch coached. "That kid thinks you walk on water."

Great. Tessa would be pleased to hear the word was spreading about Mogul Ryders, and all the more annoyed he hadn't informed her about the event. She'd never understand his reason. Hell, he didn't even fully understand why he couldn't get his head on straight and go see the competition.

"We'll be back in town the day after tomorrow. The games will still be going on."

"Cool. I'll tell everybody you'll put in an appearance. See you later, old man."

"Wait—"

Shawn hung up before Mitch could say he wouldn't be there. He'd send Tessa to do her marketing thing, but he had no intention of confronting his lost dreams just yet.

Still, knowing he couldn't compete in today's games hurt less now than it had a week ago. And he couldn't help but think he owed his greater peace of mind to a certain business dynamo in high heels.

He folded the phone and set it on the old-fashioned sink.

Would he still forge ahead with his new revisit-the-past-with-Tessa plan knowing she'd be mad when she found out about the snowboard competition in Lake Placid?

Hell, yes.

After all, he and Tessa were the originators of erotic truth or dare—the emphasis being on the dare half.

Why play it safe now?

IT TOOK every ounce of effort she possessed to drag herself downstairs for breakfast. Mitch had knocked on her door at the crack of dawn, but Tessa had refused to come out until nine o'clock. Not even the enticement of new snow could draw her from her bed any earlier.

Winding her way through the old house toward the kitchen, she caught snatches of conversation and Mitch's laughter along with the beeping of a microwave and the burble of a coffeepot.

Tessa hastened her step at the thought of caffeine.

"Morning." Mitch grinned and saluted her with a metal spatula in between flipping pancakes. The floral apron tied around his waist only accented the sheer masculinity of his six-foot-plus frame. "Mrs. Nash put me in charge of the grill when I started getting underfoot."

Their hostess smiled as she hustled around the kitchen in a Shetland sweater and corduroys. "I always got my husband involved in the kitchen." She winked at Tessa and whispered, "It's good to get them used to it early on."

Mitch hummed a bar from "Jingle Bells" and didn't seem to notice.

Mrs. Nash pulled out a sturdy ladder-back chair from the table. "Have a seat. Let us wait on you."

Tessa hesitated, accustomed to fending for herself. "I'll just get a cup of coffee."

"Cream or sugar?" Mitch called, reaching for the coffeepot.

Was she being grumpy, or was Mitch being extra nice to her? She wasn't prepared to deal with Mitch at his most charming.

"Neither." She sank into her chair and submitted to the combined energy of cheery morning people. Surely Mitch didn't have any designs on her.

He'd made sure they hauled tail out of Lake Placid specifically to avoid traveling down that road.

"So Mitch tells me you're doing a promotional tour?" Mrs. Nash called over her shoulder as she dug an electric juicer out from under a low cabinet. "Thank you for the oranges, by the way. I can't wait to try one."

Mitch set a cup of coffee in front of Tessa before she could respond. "Drink this. You'll feel better."

Oh, God. He was being extra nice.

Tessa was in way over her head.

Mrs. Nash admired the oranges while she plugged

in the juicer. "They smell so good!" She turned on the machine, rendering conversation impossible for a few moments.

Thank goodness. Tessa didn't usually talk for the first hour after she woke up. Because she worked late hours, she tried to schedule meetings for the afternoon so she could spend mornings doing less brain-intensive tasks.

She definitely wasn't ready to face Mitch behind the stove, his broad shoulders dominating Mrs. Nash's old-fashioned country kitchen. With his clean-shaven jaw and his metal spatula, he looked like the kind of man who could not only curl her hair with his kisses but could also be a stable, responsible guy.

Tessa knew better.

By the time the juicer stopped, she'd begun to feel marginally human again. She caught Mitch's eye as he set a plate of pancakes in front of her.

"I thought we'd head to Plattsburgh today," she confided as he leaned over her.

His body generated warmth, igniting a hunger the pancakes wouldn't come close to satisfying.

"Sounds good to me." His voice conveyed an intimacy beyond the words. An answering shiver tripped through her.

He moved to the stove. "I think it's a straight shot up the Northway."

Mrs. Nash gave a contented sigh. "This juice is divine! How wonderful to be a Florida girl and get to drink this all the time."

Tessa struggled to ignore the rapid rate of her heartbeat and sipped more coffee.

"Of course, being a north country native has its benefits, too," their hostess declared. "Right, Mitch?"

"There's nothing like it." He hung his apron on a brass hook and plunked down beside Tessa, his plate heaped with twice as many pancakes.

"It's so romantic to snuggle up in front of the fire on a cold winter's night." Smiling, Mrs. Nash placed a glass of juice in front of each of them. "Or walk in the snow under the stars."

Tessa couldn't argue with that. The snow and mountains had called to her spirit ever since her first trip to the Adirondacks.

Whenever she'd been out on the road for weeks at a time, besieged by people and business, she would remember what it was like to be isolated in a little cabin with the snow falling all around. Like a white veil between her and the rest of the world, there was a profound quietness about snowfall, a sense of muffling the intrusions of everyday life.

A sudden image of herself running her Internet business from a log cabin in this winter wonderland fluttered through Tessa's mind.

"But that's just me," Mrs. Nash continued, rolling up her sleeves as she began to clean up the kitchen. "I'm an Adirondacker, born and bred. I wouldn't leave here for anything."

Tessa closed her eyes to shut out the tempting image of working at her computer in sweats and slippers, a cup of cocoa in one hand and the telephone in the other. She'd never have to worry about flight delays or dressing up for client appointments again.

Out of the blue, Mitch entered her daydream to insinuate his gorgeous body between her and the computer screen. She hated to open her eyes.

"Are you tired?" Mitch's voice, no longer imagined, rumbled right through her.

Her eyes flew open. "No. I was just thinking about our trip today."

He speared another bite of pancakes. "We'll be there in an hour or so. Did you look up the addresses for where you want to go?"

Glad to redirect her thoughts, Tessa mentally reviewed her target list. "Three sporting goods stores, the daily paper, a weekly paper and a radio station."

Mitch hoped he'd misheard. Her announcement called him from his contemplation of her full lips. He set down his fork to give her his full attention. "A radio station in Plattsburgh?"

She nodded, more animated now that she'd had her coffee. "It turns out Plattsburgh is a good-size town. Less than an hour from Montreal. I wouldn't have minded hitting more radio stations there."

"Which one did you decide on?" He didn't mind going to a radio station as long as it wasn't the one where J.D. Drollette worked. How could he have forgotten about his old friend and mentor when he'd agreed to do this promotional tour?

Of course, he hadn't been doing much thinking at the time. No, he'd been too busy indulging in Tessa's kiss.

J.D. would know about the qualifying rounds in Lake Placid today.

"Let me think." Tessa drummed one finger over pursed lips. "It's an AM station. WQKI."

Mitch had no idea if that was J.D.'s home. He really

hated the thought of having their trip spoiled by the newsman who'd followed Mitch's career since college. J.D. would leak the news of Lake Placid's snowboard event, and then Mitch could kiss goodbye his notion of confronting Tessa about the tenacious heat that loomed between them.

Tessa would be too angry with him to explore the sizzle that crackled whenever they got within touching distance.

Mrs. Nash reached over his head to clear his plate. "That's my favorite station. It's hard to get the FM stations with all the mountains, but everyone gets WQKI."

An uneasiness grew in his gut. "Is that the one that's mostly talk and news?"

Their hostess cleared Tessa's plate and set it in the sink. "Uh-huh. We just love the Voice of the Adirondacks, Big J.D. I listen to his show every night."

Damn.

"What?" Tessa studied him, brow furrowed.

Had he said it aloud? He pushed his chair back. "I was just thinking we'd better get underway. Sounds like you've got a busy day lined up."

And he would have a busy day figuring out how they would avoid J.D. so he could carry out his plan to seduce Tessa.

As long as he could convince Tessa to rearrange their schedule a little bit to miss running into J.D., everything would be fine.

With a little luck, he'd be back in her bed by nightfall.

TESSA SIGHED as she looked at her itinerary for the day, hacked with arrows and cross-out marks because

Mitch wanted her to reorder the appointments. If they had followed her schedule everything would have been fine.

Instead, she was on the phone sweet-talking her contacts into changing their meeting times.

Not that she minded all that much. Being on the phone freed her from conversing with Mitch, a pastime that only reminded her more and more how much she liked him.

And wanted him.

But talking on the telephone couldn't eradicate the vision of Mitch's denim-encased thigh a few inches away.

Tessa's dreams had been haunted with thoughts of those thighs bracketing hers, of her limbs entwined with Mitch's while he...

Oh, her dreams had been incredibly good.

Too bad she would make sure they never came true. At least not while Mitch was so hung up on thrill seeking.

She could see it in his eyes last night as he'd looked through the old photos of himself snowboarding. He still craved the adrenaline rush, the adventure of his former career. And although he couldn't compete any more, his need loomed as keen as ever. Tessa didn't want to be around when he found a way to fulfill it.

His hunger for thrills and adventure would take him wherever the wind blew.

She folded up her phone and penciled in a confirmation time for the newspaper appointment.

"Sorry to mess up your plans, Tessa." Mitch glanced over at her and flashed a lopsided, conciliatory grin. "I thought we'd just stop by these places. I didn't know you called ahead and set up appointments."

"I didn't call ahead for yesterday's visits because there hadn't been enough time. Normally, I do call first."

He nodded and seemed more quiet than usual as they pulled into town.

Fortunately, the day went off without a hitch, even with all Tessa's scrambling to reorganize. Their visit to the radio station went well, despite Mitch's obvious anxiety. It struck her as odd that a man so accustomed to the spotlight would freeze up when on the airwaves.

As soon as they left WQKI, Mitch relaxed. He seemed to enjoy being the bearer of oranges at each place they went.

When they reached the newspaper, their last stop of the day, Mitch seemed in high spirits. He opened doors for her, teased her about her trench coat, and tried—in vain—to attach his troll doll pin to her collar.

His knuckles grazed her breasts, igniting a spark of liquid fire right through her clothes. Thankfully, he relented, but she had no doubt he knew just how much his touch affected her.

She'd never survive another evening of sitting in the same hotel room, no matter how much work they needed to get done. Tessa vowed to do everything herself before she wound up in his bed again.

Ines might have let her off the hook on the dare, but Tessa's sense of self-preservation still screamed at her to stay away from him.

Mitch Ryder was more than a walking aphrodisiac.

She knew from experience he possessed the power to break her heart, and she had no intention of letting that happen again.

Mitch juggled two bags of oranges while talking on her cell phone. Together, they plowed through the front doors of the town's daily paper, the *Press-Republican*.

Engrossed in Mitch's end of the conversation, Tessa didn't pay attention as she rounded a corner and slammed straight into the biggest man she'd ever seen.

"Whoa!" The giant steadied Tessa by the shoulders as if she were no more than a rag doll in a child's grasp.

Although dressed in a tweed jacket with leather patches on the sleeves, the man looked as if he'd just rolled out of bed. Dark hair stuck out from his head at every angle. Sort of Einsteinlike, but younger. A mustache covered half his mouth, but his engaging grin was still apparent.

He cleared his throat. "Excuse me, young lady. Sorry about that."

Behind her, Mitch sucked in a sharp breath of air.

The big man turned.

"Well, Mogul Mitch, as I live and breathe." The giant released Tessa with slow, methodical movements, as if he were used to moving in a way that caused the least amount of intimidation. "How the hell are you, son?"

For a moment, Mitch looked startled. He cast Tessa an apologetic look she couldn't begin to interpret, then gave the behemoth a hearty handshake.

"Hey, J.D. It's good to see you."

J.D. slapped him on the back and draped an arm like a tree limb about Mitch's shoulders. "What brought you out of the mountains?" He winked at Tessa. "You following this pretty woman?"

Tessa offered him her hand. "Tessa O'Neal. I'm the marketing executive for Mogul Ryders Snowboards."

"J.D. Drollette, ma'am, at your service." He released Mitch to shake Tessa's hand. "I heard about the new company. Sounds like a good idea."

"We were at the radio station this morning," Mitch announced. "I thought we might run into you over there."

"My show is on in the evening," J.D. explained. "I usually drop by the paper first to see if the folks over here have any big news in the works."

The Voice of the Adirondacks. Tessa thought his name had sounded familiar. Mrs. Nash called him Big J.D. for a reason.

On the heels of that thought came the realization that Mitch knew darn well when this man's show was on the air. And he had purposely tried to avoid seeing him by having Tessa rearrange their whole day.

Thinking to save Mitch from a lengthy encounter with a man he must not want to see, Tessa looked at her watch. "I'm sorry, J.D., but we have an appointment with the news editor now. We'd better be going."

Mitch nodded. "It was nice to see you—"

"Now wait a minute." J.D. scratched his head. "I'm headed down to the qualifiers today, Mitch. Why aren't you there? You afraid that mountain's going to come after you again?"

Qualifiers?

Mitch gave a halfhearted laugh. "You know my career on the slopes is over."

"The doctors tell you so?" J.D. frowned.

Mitch nodded as he rocked back and forth on his heels. "I've got to be careful not to jar my knee or spine again. I could do some real damage next time."

Tessa wondered if he'd shared so much about his accident with anyone before.

"I'd say it was pretty damn serious last time." J.D. shook a meaty finger at Mitch. "You should listen to your doctors, Mitch. But don't let that keep you away from a sport you love. You could teach the newcomers a thing or two about showmanship. It's not half as much fun commentating these things now that you're not out there.

"You're a marketing consultant." The giant turned his attention toward Tessa. "I'm surprised you didn't want to put Mogul Ryders out in front of the crowd at Lake Placid today. Seems to me you'd have a ready-made audience for your product."

It seemed that way to Tessa, too. Hadn't she asked Mitch point-blank if the event Shawn mentioned last night had to do with snowboarding?

Of course she had.

And Mitch had lied.

No matter how much Tessa might wish their relationship could be different, she couldn't change the fact that eight years later, Mitch was still playing games with her.

MITCH DIDN'T NEED to steal a glance across the truck cab to know Tessa's face would still be etched with a frown.

She was furious.

Although she'd carried on a conversation with J.D. pleasantly enough, a certain brittleness in her carriage screamed anger to a man wary of her well-concealed moods.

Ever the professional, she said nothing about the qualifiers before their meeting with the news editor, and Mitch hadn't had time between their meetings to apologize.

Mitch felt like a heel. Which, of course, he was.

Not that he was scared of the mountain, as J.D. said. Hell, Mitch looked for a reason to get on his board every day. He did small-time tricks to amuse himself, always careful not to let himself get too out of control. But he'd never be able to seek the full thrill of the mountain again.

The knowledge ate away at him.

Inside, he feared he'd be a failure, no matter how much Mogul Ryders succeeded. Would he ever be fulfilled with life as a staid businessman?

Not likely.

But if he could substitute the thrill of the mountains with the thrill of Tessa O'Neal, maybe being a staid businessman wouldn't be so bad.

In fact, it had distinct possibilities.

As they drove in silence looking for the accommodations Mitch had reserved, memories of Tessa's bedrumpled hair and throaty voice taunted him. Her peach-slicked full lips seemed to beckon from across the truck cab, even though they frowned in annoyance.

He had to think of something to make her forgive him. It would kill him if he had to keep his hands off her for even one more night. In fact, the more that he thought about the thrill of Tessa, the thrill of the mountain seemed less appealing.

Why hadn't he seen it before?

As they crunched into the gravel driveway of another countryside bed-and-breakfast, inspiration struck in the form of a snowfall. A plan came to him with the force of a north country blizzard—a surefire way to soften Tessa's heart so they could explore the fireworks between them.

"So what do you think, Tessa?" He pointed toward a gently rolling hill near the stately inn. "Are you up for a toboggan ride?"

7

Two TOE-NUMBING hours later, Tessa was soaked to the skin right through her trench coat, drained of any anger she might have felt.

No matter how much she resented Mitch playing games with her, she was a longtime sucker for tobogganing, and he knew it.

Kneeling behind her upended sled, she lobbed snowballs at Mitch. Her toboggan made a perfect shield for the icy missiles he launched at her.

Throwing things at him had ended up being wonderfully therapeutic for her annoyance.

Snow fell on her and Mitch like a damp white blanket, draping them in an icy bed and saturating the uncovered topknot of her hair.

Still, she couldn't seem to give up and go inside. For one thing, she hated to lose a snowball fight. And for another, she knew she'd jump him as soon as her fingers thawed enough to grab him.

She'd tried to refrain from seducing him, hadn't she? No matter how much she'd fought against it, the time had come to admit to herself she wasn't over him. Maybe the mature thing to do would be to face her attraction to Mitch instead of denying it at every turn.

She peeked over her toboggan long enough to catch a glimpse of him packing his next rounds of ammunition some ten feet away. Clad in a red ski jacket and wet black jeans, Mitch looked way too good for a mere mortal to resist.

Soft snow fell on his dark hair and eyelashes. A five o'clock shadow made him look dangerous in spite of the pitiful white wall surrounding him that he pretended was a snow fort.

Fascinated, she watched as his hands molded another snowball and imagined what it would feel like when he molded her flesh with those same hands. The shiver that shook her whole body had nothing to do with the wind chill factor.

She wanted him so badly she ached.

No matter that he had lied to her to get her out of Lake Placid, Tessa hungered for him as much as ever. In fact, her heart had softened toward Mitch once she realized he wasn't ready to face the sport he used to excel at. It made perfect sense to her, even though she would have preferred him to be more forthright about the snowboard competition.

Too bad a vulnerable Mitch was ten times harder to resist than his usual swaggering self.

"I see that blond head," he called, not even looking up from his careful construction of a small armory. "If you have half the sense you pretend to, woman, you'd better duck."

Maybe she needed to seek some thrills of her own for once.

She raised herself, leaving the safety of her toboggan wall. "I don't know, Mitch. I'm not feeling as scared as I was." Slowly, she lifted frozen fingers to the clips that barely held her damp tresses in place, ready to take the biggest gamble of her life. "I might just ditch the hairpins altogether and give you a real target."

The half-packed snow in his hands crumbled to the ground. He watched her, still and quiet across the clearing. White flakes rained down around them. The hushed patter of the snow's fall only intensified the silence.

"You're ditching the hairpins." He repeated her words carefully, as if he wanted to clarify them.

No doubt he was just as surprised by her actions as she felt.

"That is, if you are interested." Her frozen fingers stalled as she released the final clip that held her damp locks in place. She didn't think she could go through with this if he didn't demonstrate a small amount of willingness.

"Honey, I've been interested since you rolled a bag of oranges into my hot tub." He stepped over the low wall of his snow fort and paused. "But you've been pretty determined not to notice."

"I'm not the one who lit out of Lake Placid two days ago like a Mogul Ryder at the sound of a gun." Her heart hammered her chest.

She'd never decided to seduce a man before. Part of her increased cardiac function could be ascribed to nervousness, but most of it had to do with her acute case of lust. She wanted Mitch like she'd never wanted anything in her life.

She just needed one more night with him. A chance to revisit her fantasies. Maybe, once she'd satisfied the sharp hunger for him, she'd be able to move on with her life.

"I figured you'd hop the first flight back to Miami if

you thought I had designs on your oh-so-professional person." He moved closer, shrinking the space between them to negligible inches.

"My plane doesn't leave for four more days." Her voice caught on a breathy note. Why hadn't she thought up this plan before? It was perfect.

Maybe the years she'd spent away from him, combined with the abrupt end of their relationship, had intensified her memory of him. Tonight she'd be able to demystify the man she'd imbued with the lovemaking prowess of a god. Either that or she'd have the most sizzling sex she'd ever experienced.

"Four more days?" He pulled her against him, fitting her curves to his body like Spandex.

"Uh-huh." Her come-hither approach faltered at his touch.

He tunneled his gloved fingers into her damp tresses and tilted her head. "That means four days of letting your hair down?"

As she nodded, the soft caress of his leather-encased fingers teased her scalp.

"Four days of playing and having fun," he clarified.

How could he dictate to her when she had been the one seducing him?

"We'll have to work on business some of that time," she reminded him.

The leather palm trailed over her ear to cup her cheek. "Work will be a lot more fun from now on, Tessa."

He leaned closer, and her eyes drifted shut in anticipation of his kiss. She licked her lips, ready to mate with his mouth in the most elemental way.

Instead of receiving his kiss, she found her ear receiving his words. "But we need to get inside first."

She blinked and looked around, stunned to realize they were still outdoors despite her soaring body temperature. "Good idea."

Mitch stroked his hands down the length of her thighs and around her waist. "I'll send someone out for the sleds. I'm not wasting a minute of you in let-your-hair-down mode."

Tugging her by the hand, he led the way to the bed-and-breakfast. Tessa hurried to keep up, eager to finish what they'd started now that she'd committed herself to being with Mitch for the next four days.

Numbly, she listened to him instruct one of the kids on staff to retrieve their toboggans. Somewhere in the back of her mind she heard him request hot cocoa in his bedroom. But all she could think about was peeling off Mitch's clothes and allowing her hands to touch every inch of him. She only hoped her fingers thawed enough by then to take full advantage.

"C'mon, Tessa." Mitch whispered the words in her ear, his husky tones rasping over her senses as he pulled her toward the stairs.

Maybe because they had paused to indulge in a kiss on the stairs, their cocoa arrived at their door the same time they did. Thankfully, the girl who delivered it seemed aware of the undercurrents in the room. She ditched the drinks, tray and all, and shut the door behind her.

"So I guess it's just us," Mitch observed, looking around the spacious bedroom. "No interruptions." His gaze locked on Tessa. "No one to tell you you're making a mistake."

A shiver trembled through her. Gooseflesh spread over her skin. She didn't think she could stand it if he turned noble on her now.

"Not even you?" She had to admire him for giving her an out. But she wouldn't take it. She couldn't leave if she wanted to.

"Especially not me." He stepped closer but didn't touch her. "I'm the last person you should listen to when it comes to whether or not to sleep with me."

"Oh?"

"I'll steer you toward the sheets every time." He lifted his hand to snake around the back of her neck, underneath her hair.

"Oh." She swore she could feel the steam rise from her clothes as his words heated her body.

He pulled her closer, urging her forward until she pressed against him. Lifting her damp mane, he brushed a warm kiss over her neck.

Her legs turned soft and boneless, but his arms stole around her waist to support her. She turned her head, blindly seeking his lips and the taste of him.

But he did not kiss her so much as savor her. His tongue flicked the corner of her mouth, teasing her with the promise of a greater consummation. His hands worked the belt of her coat, freeing the knot and bringing their bodies that much closer together.

"Mitch, please," she urged, hungry to be closer, to experience more of him.

"You're so cold, honey." He squeezed her fingers and rubbed the palms of her hands with his own. "Why didn't you tell me?"

"I don't feel cold," she grumbled between kisses,

unwilling to play patient to his doctor. "I'm sure you could warm me up if you gave it a little thought."

Gently, he nipped her lower lip with his teeth. "I've got just the thing."

He tugged her coat off her shoulders and pushed her toward the bathroom.

"Is there a heater in here?" she asked. She wouldn't mind a quick blast of sauna heat.

"Even better. A shower."

Tessa stopped. "I'm not getting in the shower." That would delay their lovemaking by at least ten minutes.

"I dare you." His hands skated down her shoulders to the buttons on her blouse.

Her breath caught and held for one long moment as he popped the first button free. Once she'd managed to gulp a little oxygen again, she managed, "You think you can still coax me into doing what you want by issuing a dare?"

He smoothed one finger over the new terrain of flesh his work had uncovered.

Tessa's heart rate surged in answer.

He bent to kiss the bared valley between her breasts, then breathed his answer over her skin. "I think you still want a thrill as badly as I do."

Her breasts tightened and peaked. Her flesh tingled with wanting him.

This man knew her much, much too well.

"Maybe I do, just this once." She tugged his shirt from his jeans, up a lightly furred chest and over muscular arms.

He stood before her, bare-chested and perfectly sculpted.

"More than once." He plucked her damp silk blouse from her shoulders and turned to start the shower spray. "I'm a thrill-seeker, Tessa. Remember?"

Water beat a pulsing rhythm against the tile. Steam filled the bathroom, and moist heat wrapped around them.

"This is the kind of thrill you can seek all you want." She moved toward him, eager to plaster herself against that incredible chest.

He fingered her lemon-colored bra strap. "Thrills encased in neon yellow are all the better. Who knew you were hiding such audacious underwear beneath those navy suits?"

She murmured his name, too hungry to discuss lingerie. She'd been denied his touch for far too long.

Instead of pulling her to him, however, Mitch lifted her by the waist and stood her in the tub.

Hot water battered her body like an explosion of heated darts. Her lace bra and twill trousers molded to her body in the sudden downpour.

By the time she adjusted to the surprise shower and opened her eyes, Mitch had moved the curtain aside to join her. Completely—and deliciously—naked, he slapped a condom on the soap dish.

"Oh, my." She'd forgotten about birth control. Just as she'd forgotten how spectacular this man looked underneath his clothes. Time must have dulled her memory. "Good thing you came prepared."

"I wouldn't call it prepared. More like hopeful." Mitch cradled her cheek with one palm. "You don't mind?"

She caught herself staring at the most male part of

him. "No. I don't mind. I'm just trying to decide how much of a thrill I can handle."

He reached for her hips and drew her against him, fitting them together like two pieces of a long unfinished puzzle. Finding the zipper of her slacks, he parted the fabric and eased the garment down her hips. The slacks dropped the rest of the way to her feet on their own, soaked from their impromptu shower.

She could have stood there forever, reveling in the half-forgotten joy of his body against hers, if she hadn't wanted him inside her so badly. But no matter how heady the sensation of all that male muscle steeped in the heat of the shower, Tessa hungered for more.

Her hands roved over him with restless energy, urging him closer to taking what they both wanted. He backed her against the tile wall, his body shielding hers from the relentless spray of the water.

With one thumb, he lifted her bra strap from her shoulder, easing it down her arm. A shudder swept through her, born of anticipation and need.

"Warm enough yet?" His mouth hovered over her collarbone, above the place where her strap had recently rested.

Liquid heat pooled in her womb, yet chills broke out all over her flesh. She shook her head.

His lips covered her skin in a stifled groan. His teeth nipped her. His tongue laved her in a path that wandered from her neck to her chest. He paused to cup a breast in each hand, then raked the stubble of his cheek over the soft mounds.

Tessa's knees buckled, but his thigh braced her against the cool tiles. Her fingernails scraped the smooth surface of the wall, looking for a place to hold onto in a world suddenly tipped sideways.

But Mitch was her only anchor, her mainstay in a slippery downpour. She sank her fingers into his shoulders and hoped she wouldn't fall.

He tipped her face to his and brought his mouth down upon hers, rewarding her with the kind of mind-drugging kiss they'd been too scared to share before now. Gladly she gave herself over to him, parting her lips beneath the coaxing of his.

It had never been like this before. They had made love eight years ago, but as incredible as their coupling had been back then, it had never tilted her world on its axis and demanded everything from her.

"More." He whispered the word among his kisses, a single command she had no power, no desire, to deny him.

With languid grace she inched her leg up the outside of his, raising her knee until it grazed the top of his thigh. She hooked her foot around him, locking him against her.

The thrum of the water drowned out the beating of her heart in her ears, but she felt the blood surge through her in an equally driving rhythm.

Mitch's hand slid over her shoulder and down to her hip. He trailed a slick path over her thigh and to the inside of her leg until at last one knuckle grazed the folds of her inner flesh.

Her moan was lost in the noise of the water, but she felt the vibration of it down to her toes. With one finger, Mitch teased her, working the bud of her desire to the point of teeth-grinding release and ceasing.

She might have complained had he not started all

over again in his quest to undo her. Only this time, the build-up was twice as fast and three times as powerful. In a flash, the white heat was upon her again, demanding completion.

He reached for the soap dish and the foil packet that rested there. She manacled his wrist.

"So help me, you'd better keep touching me." She whispered the words on a breathy gasp and pointed his hand to the part of her that needed him most.

Temporarily appeased by the measured strokes of his fingers, Tessa tore open the packet and rolled the condom down Mitch's taut length.

His sharp intake of breath scarcely gave her time to brace herself. He entered her in a swift stroke that seemed to reach to the core of her being. For a long moment, he held himself there, deep inside her.

She made the mistake of looking up. Her gaze crashed into his, startling her from the physical submersion in their union. In that instant, an emotion passed between them, deep and binding and too dangerous to contemplate.

"Mitch."

His name on her lips called him from his intense contemplation. His fingers sank into the soft flesh of her buttocks, pulling her more fully around him. He withdrew from her, only to sink more deeply inside of her. With slow strokes he drew her into a vortex of keen sensation. Then he increased his pace, and she careened over the edge in a deluge of bone-melting spasms.

He groaned his fulfillment, claiming her in the most elemental way.

As they held each other in the cleansing shower of

warm water, Tessa didn't dare think about what their union meant on a deeper level. Now more than ever, she feared she would never work this man out of her system.

But she had four glorious days to try.

The Harlequin Reader Service® — Here's how it works:

Accepting your 2 free books and gift places you under no obligation to buy anything. You may keep the books and gift and return the shipping statement marked "cancel." If you do not cancel, about a month later we'll send you 4 additional novels and bill you just $3.57 each in the U.S., or $4.24 each in Canada, plus 25¢ shipping & handling per book and applicable taxes if any.* That's the complete price and — compared to cover prices of $4.25 each in the U.S. and $4.99 each in Canada — it's quite a bargain! You may cancel at any time, but if you choose to continue, every month we'll send you 4 more books, which you may either purchase at the discount price or return to us and cancel your subscription.

*Terms and prices subject to change without notice. Sales tax applicable in N.Y. Canadian residents will be charged applicable provincial taxes and GST.

If offer card is missing write to: Harlequin Reader Service, 3010 Walden Ave., P.O. Box 1867, Buffalo NY 14240-1867

GET FREE BOOKS and a FREE GIFT
WHEN YOU PLAY THE...

SLOT MACHINE GAME!

Just scratch off the silver box with a coin. Then check below to see the gifts you get!

YES! I have scratched off the silver box. Please send me the 2 free Harlequin Temptation® books and gift for which I qualify. I understand I am under no obligation to purchase any books, as explained on the back of this card.

342 HDL DRNE

142 HDL DRNU
(H-T-10/02)

FIRST NAME

LAST NAME

ADDRESS

APT.#

CITY

STATE/PROV.

ZIP/POSTAL CODE

| 7 | 7 | 7 | Worth **TWO FREE BOOKS** plus a **BONUS** Mystery Gift! |

Worth **TWO FREE BOOKS!**

Worth **ONE FREE BOOK!**

TRY AGAIN!

Visit us online at www.eHarlequin.com

DETACH AND MAIL CARD TODAY!

8

STILL DRIPPING from his shower, Mitch dug through his overnight bag for clean clothes by the half-light of dawn. He moved slowly, not out of any fear that he would wake Tessa but because their night together had worn him out.

He ran a towel over his hair and wondered for the tenth time why Tessa had forgiven him so readily yesterday. She'd known he had lied about the snowboard event in Lake Placid this week, yet she'd said nothing.

At first he thought maybe she remained silent because it hadn't been a big deal. After all, he was in charge of Mogul Ryders and he had the last say in how his business got promoted. So why should she mind?

But while he had been in the shower—during the spare moments when he hadn't been reliving the last time he'd stood on those same tiles—he'd realized the truth. The real reason Tessa hadn't stayed angry with him was that she felt sorry for him.

J.D. had been quick to reveal Mitch's reluctance to revisit the mountain scene. Tessa had obviously excused Mitch's lie out of some noble sense of kindness.

The knowledge aggravated him, but not as much as it might have if he didn't have memories of the previous night to soothe his pride.

Tugging on his boots, he peered at her. She was all

wound up in her blankets, one arm flung over his pillow as if she sought him still. She looked so innocent, so vulnerable, so totally different from last night.

He had forgotten what it had been like to share a bed with Tessa O'Neal. And she called *him* a thrill-seeker? This woman lived on adrenaline as much as he did. She just sought it in different places. Much more interesting places.

He could learn a lot from her.

But to lay beside her any longer this morning would only make him wish for impossible things. That she didn't pity him for losing his place in the spotlight. That she wouldn't leave in three more days. That he was the kind of man who could give her what she needed.

Right now, she needed to rest, and Mitch needed to work off the restless energy that plagued him despite his physical exhaustion. After pulling on a few more thermal layers, Mitch grabbed his keys and went downstairs to seek his snowboard.

A few tricks in the fresh snow might be just the thing he needed to get his mind off the sexiest blond to ever don a trench coat.

TESSA PUSHED a strand of snarled hair out of her face and glared at the clock—9:00 a.m. The telephone screeched again and again.

Who would dare to call her at 9:00 a.m.?

She knew it wasn't her client, because he was right next to her—or at least he had been. Mitch's side of the bed was cold and lonesome.

Reaching for the phone in case it might be her client

after all, Tessa groaned in time with the aches all over her body. "Hello?"

"Now that is very interesting." The musical Latin accent couldn't hide the self-satisfied tone of Ines's voice on the other end of the line.

Tessa sighed and eased back into her pillow. "What's very interesting?"

"That I rang your room all night and got no answer, yet when I ring Mitch Ryder's room first thing this morning, a very groggy sounding Tessa picks it up. May I assume you caved on the dare after all?"

Depended which dare she was talking about. Tessa had definitely fulfilled Mitch's every dare last night....

"It's a long story," she managed, finally.

"Mmm. Too long, if you ask me." Bracelets chimed across the airwaves, and Tessa could imagine Ines pointing a red-painted fingernail to punctuate her words. "Eight years is plenty long for even the most stubborn of lovers to work things out."

"We're not lov—" Tessa clamped her mouth shut, realizing she couldn't honestly refute Ines's words anymore.

"Ah. You see? You were lovers then, and you are lovers now. The two of you cannot resist one another if you are in the same state."

A fact Ines had known all too well.

"What can I say, o' wise one?" Tessa combed a weary hand through her hair. "You saw it coming before I did."

"Would you like to know what Madame Ines predicts for you next?"

"You hang up so I can go back to sleep?"

"That depends. Is Mitch there now?"

Tessa wondered which response would get Ines to leave her alone. It was much too early to plot against a determined cupid, however, so she went with the truth. "No."

"Then you are stuck talking to me, *chica*. And I predict your relentless Mogul Ryder won't let you go this time."

The sentiment warmed Tessa for a moment. She allowed herself an instant to daydream about that particular scenario before rising out of bed to face the reality of the day.

"For a tough-as-nails businesswoman, you sound suspiciously like a romantic, Ines." Tessa smiled as she crossed Mitch's room, thinking of Ines in her sturdy armor of silver and jewels.

Ines harrumphed, no doubt insulted. "I will probably fire a few slackers today to make up for it."

"Yeah, right." Tessa sat in the chair by the windows, amazed her body could be so sore from activities that had brought her incredible pleasure. "I've got to track down Mitch and get to work now. Did you want anything else besides giving me a hard time?"

"*Si.* Check out the weather channel. There are serious storms headed your way, and I am worried about you being on the road today."

Bad storms should probably concern her, but Tessa savored mountain weather enough to feel a jolt of anticipation. Storms in Miami meant rain or maybe a hurricane. But a winter storm in the Adirondacks surely meant a blizzard.

The cord for the window blinds dangled a few feet from her fingertips, so Tessa leaned forward to pull it and see how the sky looked so far. Blinding white light filled the room as she was treated to a gorgeous view of the woods behind the bed-and-breakfast, the big toboggan hill, and Mitch Ryder showing off on his snowboard.

Doing aerial tricks.

With his bad knee.

Fear knifed through her. What was he thinking?

"I've got to go, Ines." She scrambled across the room to find her trench coat. "I'll call you tomorrow when we get back to the Hearthside."

"But—"

Tessa hung up the phone, too angry and worried about Mitch to explain herself to her friend. Belting the still damp coat around her waist, she stepped into a pair of Mitch's sneakers and tromped down the stairs.

She made it all the way to the back door, ready to rail at him for risking his health and mobility, when it occurred to her what she was doing.

Tossing aside her dignity to tell Mitch what he didn't want to hear.

Why should she run to take care of him when he obviously didn't care about himself enough to follow his doctor's orders? This was precisely the kind of thing Mitch had never wanted from her. His life wasn't about roots or about living among people who cared about him.

Mitch was more concerned with where his next thrill was coming from. He wouldn't thank her to run to his rescue when he was eager to risk his neck.

Moreover, Tessa would be a fool to fall into the old trap of thinking they meant something to each other after one night together.

She relinquished the doorknob and turned to go to her room. The untied shoelaces of Mitch's sneakers slapped the worn carpet of the corridor, a rhythmic reminder of her folly. She mustered a smile for some other patrons of the hotel, feeling more than a little silly in a rumpled trench coat with a bad case of bed head.

Thankfully, Mitch would never know how close she had come to violating their decision to get over one another. She would stick to their plan to keep it simple and ignore Mitch's attempts to do himself in.

It shouldn't matter to her.

But if Mitch thought he was going to seduce his way into her bed again, he had another think coming. She couldn't risk her heart that way, couldn't allow herself to care too much again. Because come Sunday, she planned to start a new business, move on with her new life and forget all about Mitch Ryder.

IF NOT for the exchange of a few heated glances across the truck cab, Mitch might have thought Tessa had forgotten everything that transpired between them the night before. Ever since they'd pulled out of the bed-and-breakfast that morning, she'd been as cool and reserved as ever.

She'd looked ready to tackle Wall Street or anything else that got in her way when she'd arrived in the lobby with her briefcase and neat wool suit, her hair tamed into perfect submission all pinned to her head. Damned if he knew how, but she'd even managed to press out all yesterday's wrinkles from her trench coat.

Consequently, Mitch had been too surprised by her

regression into boardroom barracuda to address what had happened between them.

Somewhere between Lyon Mountain and Loon Lake, during one such accidental exchange, Mitch decided to broach the topic.

Hell, what more did he have to lose with her?

"Call me cynical, but it looks to me like you've got the worst case of last-night regret I've ever seen." He drummed his thumbs on the steering wheel, wishing her response didn't mean as much to him as it did.

She made a strangled little noise that might have been surprise at his bluntness. Then she shuffled the papers in her lap. "You sound as if you've seen that sort of thing a number of times."

"Not among women *I've* dated, of course. But sometimes with girlfriends of my buddies...you know how that is."

"But your women never have regrets?"

Bolstered by the teasing note in her voice, Mitch flashed her a wink. "You didn't see that satisfaction guaranteed stamp on my boxers?"

Tessa snorted. "If I'd known where the warranty was located I would have never let you in the shower naked."

"Honey, you're a returning customer. I didn't think you'd need it." Damn, it felt good to have her by his side again. If only he had a clue what he'd done wrong this time.

She shook her head, the smile slipping from her lips. "I didn't. And I think you know I don't have any complaints about my level of satisfaction last night."

"Well, that's something, anyway."

His thumbs picked up the pace of his steering-wheel drum solo. He told himself to wait, to see what she would say if he gave her a little time. No matter what she said, something was obviously bugging her this morning.

Against his will, words popped out before he could stop them. "I'm sorry I didn't tell you about the snowboard event in Lake Placid this week, Tessa." Maybe she was still miffed about that?

"Did I damage the PR campaign by not giving Mogul Ryders any visibility there?" He hated feeling guilty.

Tessa shook her head, sending wisps of blond hair dancing across the shoulders of her trench coat. "It would have helped you to be there, but we'll still get the word out."

The sincerity in her voice told him that wasn't what was eating at her today.

He expelled a breath he hadn't realized he'd been holding. Even though he knew Tessa had forgiven him for the lie, he had been secretly afraid he had somehow blown their whole promotional strategy because of a stupid reluctance to hang out in a scene he would never be part of again.

"How big was the event, anyway?" Tessa shifted in her seat, turning toward him for the first time since he'd crawled out of the bed they'd shared last night.

"They only had snowboarding and skiing. The mountains around here aren't big into sno-cross or motorcycle events."

"Sno-cross?"

"Snowmobile racing."

"Did they have a slope-style event?"

Mitch felt every muscle in his body tense. Obviously Tessa remembered his favorite area of competition—slope style was snowboarding that incorporated jumps and tricks and was scored on overall impression of a run.

He took a deep breath, forcing himself to relax. "Lake Placid always draws a big crowd with slopestyle games. They had super pipe and half pipe competitions, too."

"What does Shawn compete in?"

"He does it all." Mitch tried to hide his pride in his best student. "Of course, he's no Mitch Ryder."

"Of course not." She conceded the point with an indulgent smile. "But if he is talented, we ought to keep him in mind as a potential spokesperson."

"Sort of a new and improved version of me?" He hadn't meant to sound bitter, but he heard it in his words as clearly as she must.

Thankfully, she ignored his remark and scribbled some notes on her yellow legal pad. "The spokesperson slot could be like a legacy to hand down every few years. The Mogul Ryder crown, so to speak."

As they jounced over a bump in the winding mountain road, her pencil broke. She tore through her purse for a replacement. "You should really host an event, Mitch. We could have a competition every five years, so it wouldn't be as expensive as yearly." She chattered away as she dug through her handbag, then fell into silence once she had a writing instrument in hand again.

The only sound in the truck was Tessa's new pencil scratching along the surface of the paper in a furious attempt to keep up with her creative outburst.

"I don't know, Tessa."

The scratching slowed. Then stopped altogether.

"You don't know what?"

He downshifted as they passed through a shaded section of the narrow highway. Now that the sun was starting to set, he feared some parts of the road would be cold enough to freeze.

"I don't know if I'm ready to hand over my name to someone else." She would think he was being petty. Hell, *he* was pretty sure he was being petty. "It's one of the few things I earned that will endure."

"It will endure even longer with people to carry it on for you."

He grinned. "Sort of like children?"

Was it his imagination or did she blush? She tapped her pencil against the pad of paper in a monotonous rhythm.

"Sort of. Only you'll be guaranteed grateful off-spring who share your interests."

"Which is a lot more than my father got."

"That's not true. You are a grateful son." She sounded indignant on his behalf. "And both you and your dad love sports."

"A lot of people don't consider snowboarding much of a sport."

"It's in the Olympics."

Mitch laughed to think of what his dad's response to that one would be. "So is ballroom dancing."

Tessa didn't even crack a smile. "What *would* make him proud?"

"He thinks I should have played baseball. Accord-ing to him, it's not only more American, it's also the best sport to choose if you're not overly athletic."

"Not athletic?" She lowered her voice to a sexy drawl. "He's never seen you in the shower."

Heat sizzled through his veins despite the snow piling around them. He tried to block out the urge to pull Tessa underneath him by recalling one of many arguments with his father. "I never conquered the four-minute mile. Dad finally threw away my football cleats and gave me a bat instead."

"And you said enough is enough and got yourself a snowboard?"

"I bought skates and wrangled a scholarship to play hockey at the University of Vermont."

Her throaty laugh warmed him. "Effectively securing your ticket away from home along with your college education. Smart man."

He allowed himself a moment to bask in her approval. Tessa might sing his professional praises to the skies in front of the media, but she had little reason to compliment him in the privacy of his truck unless she really meant it.

"The Mogul Ryder crown could be like a scholarship."

Had she been looking for an opportunity to bring up her latest scheme again?

The words sucker punched him. Maybe her compliment had been given with an ulterior motive, after all.

"It would give validation to someone who is talented." She pressed on. "By offering a lucrative endorsement contract for a prize, you increase the level of competition, which ultimately improves the whole sport."

Mitch shook his head. "You're relentless."

She flashed him her close-the-deal grin. "I don't quit."

"Except when it really matters?" He hadn't meant to say it. But there was something less personal about conversation in the truck. It was easier to talk while staring through the windshield at the snowstorm.

She stiffened. "I don't think that's fair."

"Sorry." He slowed down as they reached Loon Lake.

Tessa pointed out the store on the main road, and Mitch pulled off the street to park. They were supposed to see a sporting goods store owner in town and then hit two more spots on their way to Lake Placid.

Mitch grabbed a sack of oranges and moved to open his door. "Guess I'm just disappointed that you seem to regret last night."

She caught his arm before he could go anywhere. "I definitely don't regret last night." Her fingers flexed into his bicep as if to impress her point.

He reached across the seat and traced her jaw with his thumb. "Good."

"If I've been quiet today, it's not because I have any regrets." Her gaze narrowed by a fraction. "I was just a little surprised to wake up and see you risking your neck to show off a few tricks on the board."

Was that all? "I'm careful."

"You equate aerial stunts with being careful?" Tension threaded her voice.

At least he'd finally discovered why she'd been holding back on him this morning.

"They aren't as demanding as they look. I—"

She pressed her fingers over his mouth, silencing his words. "I don't know how you can risk your future health for a few minutes of adulation from strangers, but I know I should just respect that's the way you are."

Her fingers slid from his lips to smooth over his cheek. "I keep telling myself I shouldn't get tangled up with you again."

"Honey, getting tangled up is what we do best." He pulled her closer. As much as he wanted—needed—to keep their relationship in the safety zone of just physical, the sadness in her eyes made him want to protect her, hold her, say anything to banish the hurt. Even words that were damn near impossible to utter. "But if you've changed your mind about how we spend our last few days together, I'll understand."

"You will?"

Was it his wishful imagination, or did she look a little bit disappointed? Mitch wanted to think he had misread her mood today. "I will. I'd never want you to sleep with me if you had doubts."

She gave him a halfhearted smile.

"The only trouble is—"

"What?"

He pointed toward the window. "The trouble is we'll be lucky to find a place to stay tonight before the roads become impassable."

Tessa swiveled in her seat to peer outside. Her smile faded as she saw the windshield was already completely covered in snow.

Mitch struggled to look serious, all the while thanking God for sending a northeaster just when he needed it. "There's no way we'll make it back to Lake Placid tonight."

9

THEY HAD TO make it to Lake Placid tonight.

Tessa shivered in Mitch's front seat as he inched the truck down the interstate. After a quick promotional visit to the store in Loon Lake, they'd decided to cancel their remaining appointments and return to the Hearthside Inn before the weather got any worse.

As Tessa squinted through the onslaught of white flakes, she feared they would never get all the way to Lake Placid.

Which meant checking into another intimate bed-and-breakfast with Mitch. And pretending everything was fine when Mitch played the gallant and left her alone all night.

She didn't mean to give him the impression she regretted their time together. In truth, it took every ounce of effort not to sidle closer to him. She wanted another night in his arms, but how could she do that, knowing he would only turn around the next morning to seek a greater thrill, one that her bed couldn't provide? One she never could provide?

Despite her best effort to keep things simple, she cared about him too much already. The closer she got to him, the more power he possessed to break her heart again.

So she prayed they would make it to Lake Placid where Tessa would have the Hearthside to herself and

Mitch had his own cabin a mile up the road. She couldn't stand the thought of sleeping in another tiny roadside inn with nothing between them but a few inches of drywall.

"I haven't seen another car since we left Loon Lake," Mitch muttered. He cracked his window and reached out to help his frozen windshield wipers clear a view.

"Maybe no one else is as eager to get somewhere as we are."

"Or as eager to leave someplace behind?" Mitch didn't take his eyes off the road as he said it, but Tessa knew the question was meant for her.

Hoping to help, she leaned out her window and swiped at the encrusted snow with one gloved hand. "I told you I don't regret last night."

"Only who you spent it with."

She'd never seen this side of Mitch before, this bitterness. He was usually playful and witty, a welcome counterpoint to her more down-to-business approach to life. She wasn't quite sure how to handle his darker side.

"No. Only that we can't get along as well out of bed as we do in it." She couldn't help but correct him. When she left Lake Placid this time, she would go home knowing she'd at least been forthright with him.

"I always thought we got along great." He chanced a quick glance across the truck cab, eyes gleaming with mischief. "We both love to play in the snow."

"True enough."

"We both love neon yellow, even though you hide your penchant under navy business suits."

"Well..."

"And we both love the thrill of a new adventure."

"Wrong."

"I'm not wrong, Tessa." He peered at her, surprised. "If you're such a stick-in-the-mud, then why are you leaving your safe, respectable career while you're at the top?"

Her mouth opened but no words came out. Was she more adventurous than she realized?

Before she could refute the idea, a car heading toward them careened over the yellow line, straight into their lane.

"Look out!" Tessa called, even though Mitch was already steering the truck off the road and out of the way.

A split second later, Mitch's truck plowed into a snowbank while the out-of-control car fishtailed its way up the interstate.

"Damn!" Mitch hit the steering wheel with his fist to punctuate the word. "What the hell are people thinking to drive like that in the middle of a blizzard?"

Shaken, Tessa righted herself in her seat and sent up prayers of thanksgiving they were still alive.

"Are you okay?" Mitch unfastened his seat belt and slid beside her.

She turned to him, grateful for his cool head and smart driving. She nodded against the smooth nylon of his ski jacket and wished she could stay wrapped in his arms.

"You know I was driving as carefully as I could." His voice rasped in the quiet stillness. "I would never endanger you that way."

"I know."

"I don't seek my thrills behind the wheel of a car."

She fumbled to get her arms underneath his jacket so she could tuck herself against his chest. "I know you don't. You couldn't have been any more careful."

He stroked her hair while she listened to his heart slow down to a more steady thump. "I could have insisted we stay put today instead of risking our necks in a blizzard."

"How are we going to get out of here?" she asked. The truck hood was completely buried in a snowbank.

"With a lot of cursing."

"Can I help?"

"Not unless you know a few words that I don't." He pulled away and zipped up his jacket.

Tessa mourned the loss of his warmth, his strength. But their few quiet minutes together had helped her bring things into perspective. She had been immature and selfish to insist Mitch get them to Lake Placid in the middle of a snowstorm.

"Do you think there is any place we could stay nearby?" she ventured.

"We just passed signs for Buck Pond. There is a state park there that might have a cabin or two."

"A cabin?" Her resolve to be unselfish faltered when confronted with thoughts of spending the day ensconced with Mitch in a cozy little hideaway.

She'd never keep her hands to herself.

"I think it's the best we can hope for at this point." He pulled on his gloves and hat, then hopped out of the truck. He leaned in before closing the door. "But don't worry, Tessa. I won't bite...unless you dare me to."

Oh, God.

It was going to be a very long day if Mitch wasn't

going to behave himself. She could already feel her
hairpins itching her scalp.

MITCH THANKED GOD for snow tires and chains as he
limped down the road toward the park ranger's
house. It had taken almost an hour, but he and Tessa
had finally maneuvered the truck out of the snowbank. Although he had protested he didn't need her
help, she had insisted on taking the wheel while he
pushed. He would have never known she was a
southern girl by the way she mastered the rhythm of
stepping on the gas when he rocked the truck.

They had cheered their success when the pickup finally found some traction and bolted backward onto
the interstate. But now that Mitch was out of Tessa's
sight, he allowed himself the luxury of limping. He
had blown out his knee while pushing the truck, and
the pain knifed through him with each step toward
the ranger's house. He didn't know how he would
make it to the main road, let alone to whatever remote
cabin the state park might have available.

By the time he reached the ranger's residence, the
snow whirled around him like a cold, white cloud.
The front steps were caked with new powder while
the eaves dripped icicles. Mitch knocked on the door,
grateful for the support of the rough-hewn handrail
while he awaited an answer.

On the third try, the door swung open to reveal two
little girls with matching milk moustaches and long
brown ponytails.

"Grandpa, it's a man!" the littler one shouted as she
eyed Mitch critically. "Mister, you don't look so
good."

Mitch had to laugh at that one. This little girl didn't miss a trick.

The bigger girl elbowed her. "Just a minute, sir, while I get my grandpa."

No sooner had the two ponytails whirled around than they collided with a wiry older man who came up behind them. At barely five and a half feet, the man stood back from Mitch so he didn't have to look up at him.

"Son, what happened to you?" The old man held out a weathered hand. "Get on in here, boy, and warm up. Girls, go get our guest one of your famous chocolate-chip cookies."

Little feet raced down the hallway before Mitch could protest.

"I really shouldn't, I've got—"

"Don't be a fool, son. It's not fit for man nor beast out there." The man tugged on Mitch's elbow until he could close the door behind him.

Mitch tried to stay on the front mat so he wouldn't rain snow on the floor.

His host crossed his arms over his chest. "What can I do for you?"

The little girls returned with a plate of chocolate chip cookies and a purple plastic cup of milk for Mitch. He balanced the plate in one hand while he talked.

"My truck is parked out on the highway, but I don't want to risk driving any farther in this weather. I thought the park might have some sort of cabins I could rent for the night."

The old man snorted. "This isn't the Holiday Inn, son."

"I know, sir." Mitch wished he had sent Tessa on this mission. She would have sweet-talked them a place to stay in no time. Judging by the way the old man smiled at the ponytailed twosome, Mitch guessed he had a soft spot in his heart for pretty girls. "I blame myself for venturing out in a blizzard. I honestly had no idea it would get this bad."

"I'm not supposed to let anyone stay on state property this time of year." The old man snitched a cookie from Mitch's plate and reached for the telephone. "If you give me your name, I can call my friend in the next town over. She has a little—"

Mitch shook his head. His knee throbbed from the activity and the warmth of the cabin. "The name's Mitch Ryder, sir. But what I really need is to get out of this snowstorm before it gets any worse. I've got a friend with me—"

"Mitch Ryder?" A glimmer of recognition lit the man's eyes. "As in Mogul Mitch Ryder?"

Should he deny it? Mitch knew some of the Adirondack old-timers didn't appreciate snowboarder types on the mountains. "Yes, sir."

The weathered face split into a wide grin. "Well, I'll be! You're the hometown hero, son. Why didn't you say who you were?" He slapped Mitch's back and then ambled to another part of the house. He shouted to Mitch as he walked away. "I can't let just anybody traipse around the park this time of year, but we care for our own around here."

The sudden welcome gave Mitch an odd sense of being at home in a way he'd never experienced at his own house. He lifted the purple plastic cup to his mouth and took a drink.

"You follow snowboarding?" he called into the next room.

The man reappeared with a single silver key in his extended hand. "Ever since I got a satellite dish. You can't drag me away from the sports channels when I'm not on grandpa duty. The name's Gus Harper, by the way."

Mitch set his cup and plate on a table in the entryway, then took the key. "I won't forget it, Mr. Harper, I guarantee it."

"Call me Gus, son. That cabin isn't much but it's the closest to the road if you just drive another mile on the interstate. You can almost see it through the trees when there's not a blizzard in action."

Reaching for the door, Mitch shouted a farewell to his ponytailed hostesses. "Thanks, Gus. I won't forget I owe you a big favor." He winced as he stepped outside. His knee had grown stiff and swollen in the few minutes he had been standing still.

Gus waved out the door while his granddaughters clamped themselves to him. "Forget it! Just make a big comeback for us next year. Show all those Rocky Mountain hotshots that the east coast boys know how to ride," he shouted.

Mitch cringed at the familiar advice even as he smiled and waved goodbye. How many times had his father criticized him for not getting back on the slopes already?

He moved slowly through the swirl of snow, hoping the pain in his knee would ease if he didn't push it. Halfway to the truck he spied Ms. Madison Avenue stomping through snowdrifts in her trench coat.

"What in God's name are you doing walking

around out here in that paper bag you call a coat?" He hoped the strobe-light effect of the falling snow would conceal the fact that he was limping, because he no longer had the option of putting any more weight on his knee.

"This is a perfectly good winter coat." She plowed through the remaining snow between them and scanned him with an assessing gaze. "Where have you been? Are you hurt?"

A denial sat on his lips, ready to go. But hadn't he regretted the last time he'd lied to Tessa? "My knee is protesting the activity. I'll be fine once we get out of the cold."

She frowned. He would bet his business that a sharp condemnation sat on her lips. No doubt she wanted to tell him how foolish he had been to limp all the way to the ranger's house and back.

Instead, she sidled underneath his arm and wrapped it around her shoulders. "Lean on me." She stepped forward, bearing a portion of Mitch's weight on her slender shoulders. "Did you find a place for us to stay?"

He withdrew the key from his pocket and held it out to her. "Less than a mile up the road."

The way she smiled at him made him feel like he had just produced a magic lamp. "Thank God. Although this is a perfectly good winter coat, I find I'm getting a little cold." She kept her pace slow and even as they moved toward the truck.

Mitch wanted to protest as she led him to the passenger seat. He hated being coddled, but he could hardly pretend a strength her aching shoulders must tell her he didn't possess.

Sliding across the cold bench seat, he wished he at least had the solace of knowing they would spend the night in the same bed.

Fat chance of that.

He knew she regretted her decision to sleep with him in the first place.

The ache in his knee throbbed, a painful reminder of his imperfection. Damn, he hated feeling like a broken down old man.

Tessa O'Neal hadn't wanted him even when he was whole. What had made him think she would ever want him now?

TESSA SHOULD HAVE warmed up once they entered the little cabin on state park property. Although no fire graced the hearth, the four walls at least boasted shelter from an increasingly harsh storm. The atmosphere emanating from Mitch had dropped to a subzero chill factor, however, and she shivered at his frosty reception.

He had accepted her help from the truck with forced politeness, even though he still chose to bear more of his weight on his bad knee than to lean on her at all. Now, as he limped around the cabin, investigating what was behind each door, he scowled and cursed.

"What's the matter?" she called from the living area.

"Nothing."

"Those epithets generally signal annoyance." She shed her wet coat and hung it on a brass coat rack by the door.

He released a long-suffering sigh and pointed toward the empty firewood holder on the hearth. "We're going to be a little cold with no wood."

Mitch grabbed an ax from two hooks over the back door and muttered something about getting to work while Tessa moved closer to the fireplace and peered inside.

"...don't know how we'll start a fire with wet wood, but—"

"We don't have to." Tessa dug in her purse for a pack of matches.

He leaned on the ax like a staff, and Tessa tried to remind herself not to be too hard on a man in pain.

"What do you mean we don't have to? This isn't Miami, Tessa. We'll freeze—"

"Duraflame." She opened the fireplace doors and nodded to the chemical log inside the dark niche. "Thank goodness for modern miracles." She struck a match to three points on the paper and watched the log ignite.

"That won't keep us warm through the night," he argued, spinning the wooden handle of the ax in his palms. "That puny blaze wouldn't dry a pair of socks let alone heat the cabin until morning."

"I can see you are just itching to swing your ax and conquer the forest with your might, but let's see if the thermostat works first, shall we?"

"Thermostat?" He quit spinning the ax.

She pointed toward the dial on the wall near the kitchenette. "It's worth a shot, don't you think?" She moved to turn it up.

"I'll get it." Mitch jammed the ax on its hooks.

Tessa paused mid-stride. "I'm closer, and I'm uninjured," she said as reasonably as she knew how. "Why not let me?"

He limped over anyway, scowling her into remaining where she stood. With the turn of a dial, the low whir an electric heater became audible.

Tessa bit her tongue to keep from pointing out she could have handled it all on her own. Instead, she told herself he was only being surly because of his knee. She took a calming breath and smiled at him.

"If you put your leg up for a little while, I bet the swelling would go down. You might feel better." Sure, that was obvious information, but Mitch had apparently not thought of it.

"I thought I'd get our luggage and some oranges from the truck first. You must be getting hungry." He pivoted toward the door.

"I can get them!" She grabbed his arm and steered him toward the couch, determined to make him sit down before he fell down. "I've got a good loaf of cinnamon raisin bread I bought from the bed-and-breakfast this morning, too. I'll make us something to eat."

"Damn it, Tessa!" He shook off her arm. "I'm fully capable of getting everything myself."

What should she do with such a cranky roommate? He acted like an overtired five-year-old. "But why should you when you are in excruciating pain and I'm not? Are you being a male chauvinist pig or just a stubborn patient?"

"I'm being a gentleman." He crossed his arms and stared at her with a glare that contradicted his statement.

"Excuse me for confusing your gentleman guise for

a Neanderthal." She leaned forward, closing the distance between them to mere inches. His coat smelled like truck fuel and cold air. "I'd have better luck talking Cro-Magnon man into putting his foot up than bullheaded Mitch Ryder."

His eyes narrowed, and he unfolded his arms. The action seemed to bring them closer together, dropping a barrier that had been there moments before. "Honey, if you think Cro-Magnon man is an improvement on me, I'd be more than glad to drag you back to my cave by your hair."

"How utterly barbaric." Heat flowed through her limbs like sap in the spring. She'd never be a hip woman of the millennium if she let a remark like that turn her on.

"You started making comparisons, not me." His hands slid up her arms to mold around her shoulders. He pulled her body flush against his, giving her a vivid preview of what he had to offer. "Is it my fault that our cave ancestors knew how to end an argument?"

Tessa resisted with about as much force as a rag doll. "Does this mean you're going to start dragging me around by the hair?"

With a searching touch, he sifted through her locks and trailed his fingers over her scalp. "I think we both know those pins have been just itching to come out, Tessa."

10

MITCH COMBED his fingers through her silken locks and popped the first pin free. She sighed in his arms and wriggled closer, effectively assuring him his version of caveman games hadn't offended her.

Plunging both hands into her hair, he dispersed the remaining pins, sending them in a series of pings to the hardwood floor. He released her mouth to bury his face in the mane, relishing the scent of her. Even a thousand miles from her native state, she still smelled like sunshine.

His whole body clamored for her, drawn to her heat like a snowbird on spring break. He leaned forward, planning to scoop her in his arms, when pain lanced his right leg.

"Damn!" He swallowed the litany of other curses that rose to his lips at the sharp pain in his knee.

Tessa pulled away, her green eyes clouding in confusion for a moment before she slid underneath one of his arms to support him. "Let's get you to the couch, okay?"

He had a much better idea.

"No. I need to soak it." He steered her in the direction of the bathroom and the hot tub he had already discovered. The sparse cabin hid an extravagant luxury. "Walk me this way."

"I'm very good in the shower." She helped him

through the bathroom door. "I'd be happy to stay and help...oh, my." Her eyes locked on the whirlpool bath ensconced in a bay of floor-to-ceiling windows. Snow fell like a white curtain behind the glass.

"By all means, please stay and help." Having Tessa around for inspiration would definitely improve his condition in a hurry.

She shot him a reproving glare, but he caught the mischievous light in her eyes. "I'm not offering *that* kind of help."

Oh, but he hoped she would be. Soon.

"Then I guess I'll take whatever you are offering." He trailed one finger down her cheek. "You can be my lifeguard while I soak. Remember the buddy system?"

"I *am* very good at mouth-to-mouth." She relented. "Especially when the recipient is a hotshot snowboarder."

Now she was talking his language. His body reacted immediately, straining toward her with every pulse-thumping beat of his heart. "I'm feeling a little short of breath already," he confessed, taunted by fantasies of Tessa's lips on his. "How about a demonstration?"

She hovered closer, her eyes drifting shut. God, she was gorgeous. Mitch reached for her hips and stepped closer....

His knee buckled beneath him. Only a little, but he could tell she'd noticed by the way her eyes flew open.

Of all the damn timing.

"You'd better get in the tub." She reached for the knobs and turned on the hot water full blast. "Alone."

Mitch groaned. "We were this close to resurrecting naked Marco Polo."

Tessa tossed in a bar of soap and turned on the water jets. Bubbles frothed and grew, filling the tub faster than the water. "Don't get too sure of yourself, Mitch. I was contemplating a kiss, not swimming in the buff with you."

He grumbled as he eased his boots and socks off. "A guy's gotta start somewhere."

He focused on the task at hand—getting his knee under control so he could salvage a night with Tessa. If he couldn't keep her by his side after this week, he would at least have some incredible memories to take with him.

That notion didn't comfort him as much as it should have.

"I can usually pop this thing back into place after I soak it," he explained, shedding his jacket and unbuttoning his shirt.

"This has happened before?" She turned off the water and crossed her arms over her stodgy suit. The steam from the bath made a halo effect behind her body.

"Only once or twice since the accident."

She shook her head. "You have to take better care of yourself, Mitch. How long do you think that knee will last when you're continually jolting it out of joint?"

He shrugged. He hadn't really given it much thought.

"You need to be more careful." She moved closer to stand between his legs. She eased his shirt off his shoulders and smoothed her hands over his bare chest. "I take responsibility for today's injury, because

I urged you to get us back to Lake Placid. But what about the other times this has happened?"

"I know what you're getting at, Tessa. Point taken."

Her hands paused near his waist. "What am I getting at?"

"You don't think I should still be snowboarding."

"I don't think you should be risking your long-term health for the sake of a thrill, and if you've done this to yourself on the slopes before, then I think you ought to find a new way to generate an adrenaline rush." Her fingers slid lower, finally settling on the button of his jeans.

He captured her hands in his. "I'd prefer your brand of thrills over what I find on the slopes, any day. Maybe you should stick around so I wouldn't be injuring myself all the time."

Her eyes grew round for a moment, then she blinked several times in rapid succession. "You're just trying to guilt me into staying so I'll help you market Mogul Ryders."

He let his gaze roam her long, silky hair, her charming crooked nose and the fabulous curves encased in no-nonsense gray wool. "Honey, I'd be a fool not to try whatever it takes to make you stay."

Tessa stared at him, momentarily spellbound by the warm cocoon of steam and the sheer magnetism of the man. Could he be serious? Or was he only interested in having her around for replays of the previous night?

Tessa backed away, unaccustomed to the feeling of vulnerability he inspired. "I'll let you start soaking." She stepped toward the door, swamped by the depth of her longing for a man who possessed the power to hurt her deeply. "I'll go...peel our oranges."

She shoved her way out of the bathroom, ignoring him when he called after her. For all she knew, he only wanted her to come back in so she could help him into the tub. But she wasn't ready to face him right now. Her feelings were too jumbled, too raw.

Besides, Mitch Ryder had found his way into a tub all the other times he'd blown out his knee when she wasn't around. She didn't need to solve all his problems for him.

Still, she waited until she heard the reassuring splash of water before she moved toward the cabin's front door. She donned Mitch's ski jacket instead of her dripping trench and stepped into the blizzard.

Snow swirled in squalls and rained from the sky, filtering her vision with white spots. Through the bare trees, she could see a hint of Mitch's pickup, and she put her head down to tromp the distance between her and it.

On a whim, she pulled Mitch's cell phone out of his pocket and tried dialing Ines, but cellular communication in the Adirondacks was sketchy at best, and she couldn't get through.

Too bad, because she really needed to talk to the Wise One about this.

Reaching the pickup, she pulled out their bags and grabbed a sack of oranges. How could she be so turned around about Mitch after less than one week in his company? She trudged toward the cabin and wondered how she'd strayed so far from her original plan to stay out of Mitch's bed, and maybe confront her past before she moved on with her new life.

She'd failed miserably in that attempt. Instead of proving to herself she was over him, she seemed to be proving she cared about him as much as ever.

Because even knowing how much it would hurt to let him go at the end of the week, Tessa found herself fantasizing about spending tonight with him.

As she stumbled up the front steps of the cabin, Tessa vowed not to let her fears for the future ruin her last few nights with Mitch. She would simply savor their time together and store up as many memories as she could.

Funny, she had the feeling even Ines would have told her to do the same thing.

An hour later Mitch emerged from the bathroom, standing straight and tall on his own feet. He wore a pair of sweatpants from the bag Tessa had brought inside for him. His chest was missing a shirt, however.

Tessa thought she should probably offer to help him put one on. But selfishly, she didn't feel in any hurry to cover up this gorgeous man.

She noticed his gaze stray toward the sofa bed she'd pulled out and covered with blankets she'd found in a kitchen cabinet.

That bed kept catching her eye, too.

She still had a few dares in store for a certain thrill-seeker.

"You're transformed." She laid down her knife and a long strand of orange peel, hoping to keep their conversation on neutral ground long enough for Mitch to eat and rest his knee a little bit.

Heaven knew, he looked good enough to eat. Much

better than the supper of oranges and cinnamon bread she'd prepared.

"Good as new." He limped to the bed, obviously stiff, but not bearing the pained expression he'd worn before the soak. He held his broad hands out to the warmth of the small blaze in the fireplace.

"Your knee just slides back into place after a little while?" She gathered their makeshift plates made of paper towels and brought them over, using the double bed as a table for their meal.

"I have to twist my foot a little to coax it back in there, but eventually it works." He tore into the bread and devoured it in three bites.

"Sounds painful." She retrieved the loaf from the kitchen and passed it to him before perching on her half of the thermal blanket.

"At least it's effective."

"You never did do things the easy way, did you?" She separated her orange into precise sections.

"What do you mean by that?" He paused in his ravenous consumption of bread.

She shrugged, regretting hasty words that could reveal too much. "You could have played professional hockey after college, but you opted to take up a fledgling sport with a sketchy following. You could have executed perfect spins and jumps in more conventional snowboard routines, but you always pushed the envelope to perform tricks that were over the top. You could go to the doctor, but you'd rather contort yourself to fix your knee injuries on your own. Shall I continue?"

"You've proven your point." He held up his hands in mock surrender. "I guess I like a good challenge."

"Maybe." She stared into the flames from the chemical log.

"What do you mean maybe? Of course I like a good challenge." Grinning, he leaned forward to smooth his thumb over her cheek. "I pursued you eight years ago knowing I didn't stand a long-shot chance."

"Is that what I am? I'm a challenge for you?" Did she really want to know that he viewed her with as much affection as Whiteface Mountain? "Never mind. Don't answer that."

"Too late." He shoved his paper towel plate aside and slid closer to her. "Honey, you challenge me in ways I never knew a man could be challenged, and I'm not going to apologize for liking that."

Gently, he lifted her face to his and cupped her chin in his broad palm.

His touch brought back vivid memories of the night before. The shower. Then the bed.

Then the double dare that had involved way too much Jell-O and whipped cream.

She waited, wishing she hadn't brought up the subject. Why did she have to spoil the short time they had left by pushing him to clarify his feelings?

"I like it that I have to be on my toes with you, Tessa. When we're together, I don't think about what I've lost. I'm too busy thinking about my business and how much marketing knowledge I can gain from you. Or else I'm too busy *not* thinking about business and how much I'd like to sleep by your side all night." His hand skimmed down her neck to curl around her shoulder.

Her heart knocked against her ribs in response. She forgot to breathe.

"You've tested my patience." His voice dropped to a whisper, and the words fanned her cheek as he leaned closer.

A shiver coursed through her. She thought he'd been testing hers all these years.

"You've tested my endurance." His lips grazed her jaw.

Her eyes drifted shut as she recalled great feats of endurance on his part. Yes, she was definitely glad she'd challenged him in that particular area.

"God knows, you've tested my restraint." He kissed each of her closed eyes, calling them open again. "And I wouldn't trade a minute of it."

His words sounded sincere enough, but Tessa knew better than to trust them. She could think more clearly when he wasn't kissing her.

"You'd trade it for an adrenaline high and center stage on the slopes." She remembered too well that he'd been unwilling to give up his thirst for adventure eight years ago.

"You still hold that against me, don't you?" The accusatory tone in his voice surprised her.

"No. But between your defection and my husband's, I've pretty much learned I can't trust a man who lives for a thrill."

He made a time-out sign with his hands. "Wait a minute. Don't group me with an ex-husband, because I would never walk away from my wife."

"Fine. You wouldn't walk away from a wife, but you sure as hell know how to walk away from me." She folded her arms over her chest, needing any barrier she could scavenge between them.

"And do you think *you* could have walked away

from your career before you'd reached the pinnacle of success?" He folded his arms in return. "Care to make this a truth or dare?"

His question caught her off guard.

"Well—the situations aren't really the same." That was as much truth as she could face right now.

"They're close enough." He reached out to her, smoothing his hands over her shoulders. "You are just as much an overachiever as I am. You would never be walking away from your marketing career right now unless you had reached the top. And I didn't have the power to walk away from mine until I had achieved all I could."

"Even if it meant giving up on us." She clung to that one thought, because she didn't want to acknowledge that she understood him all too well.

Damn it, she hadn't ever been able to walk away from something until she'd mastered it. Her divorce had been hell on her, not so much because she mourned the loss of a husband who had never been right for her, but because she couldn't stand the thought of failing.

"I didn't give up on us." He tugged at her crossed arms, pulling them loose to wrap them around himself. "I asked you to come with me. Remember?"

"You knew I'd never be able to live that way. A farmer's daughter can't have a rootless existence."

"Home is where the heart is, Tessa. I think you were just too eager to start your marketing job in Florida to tie yourself to a gypsy like me."

She opened her mouth to argue.

Mitch laid one finger across her lips, shushing the rebuttal she couldn't seem to form. "It's a long time ago. Maybe we just weren't meant to be together back then."

He traced the outline of her lips with the pad of his thumb, inciting a wave of heat to pulse through her limbs. She nipped at the thumb, then relieved the slight pressure of her teeth with a delicate brush of her tongue.

Mitch watched her actions as if hypnotized. "I just want to know if we are meant to be together now." Slowly, his head dipped to her neck, where he venerated her flesh with his kisses.

His lips might have coaxed a response from her if his words hadn't frozen her in place.

Did he mean he wanted to try and have a relationship? Or was he merely issuing an invitation for the night?

"Mitch?"

He answered by sliding her suit jacket down her arms. Her silk blouse shivered in time to the shifting wool.

"Mitch?" She needed to clarify this. The health of her heart might depend on his reply.

"Mmm?" He drew her to edge of the bed and pulled her to her feet. "You ready for a round of search and rescue in that hot tub yet?"

She couldn't suppress the laughter that bubbled in her throat or the heat that swirled through her at his touch. "You're too much."

His eyes narrowed, and he settled her more firmly against his hips. He cradled her face in his hands and captured her gaze with his. "That's a sentiment I guarantee you'll be repeating before the night is through."

11

"PRETTY SURE of yourself, aren't you?" Tessa twined her fingers through Mitch's and clasped his palms.

With slow deliberation, he walked her backward, his slight limp in no way impeding his trek toward the bathroom and the still bubbling hot tub.

"I'm sure of this." He squeezed her hands, drawing her attention from the tub and to the heady temptation of his body.

She was very sure of this too. This had haunted her dreams and left her breathless and aching for Mitch in the middle of the night for longer than she'd ever admit.

They paused beside the big tub, allowing the steam to envelop them along with the snowy view.

Mitch slid his palms over the sleeves of her silk blouse. "We won't stay in the water too long." He breathed the words in her ear as his fingers sought the buttons of her shirt. "Just long enough to get slippery."

She couldn't help the little moan that escaped her lips. The man had the best ideas. What had ever made her think she didn't want a thrill-seeker? An occasional thrill suddenly seemed like a very good idea.

Tessa wriggled out of her blouse and slacks, impatient to be free of her clothes.

And slippery.

She scarcely heard Mitch's low whistle of appreciation for her pink lace bra and matching panties. She was too intent on helping him out of his sweats and boxers.

The hot tub bubbled invitingly behind them. The bathroom was lit by the shifting golden glow of a lamp beneath the water's surface.

Mitch tugged at her bra while Tessa pulled at the drawstring on his sweats. In the space of a heartbeat, he was naked and magnificent.

Before she could comment on that fact, Mitch nudged her toward the bath and helped her over the ledge of the hot tub. She squealed as she hit the hot water. Bubbles tickled her sensitive skin and licked over her in restless waves.

This was delicious madness.

Before she could change her mind or come to her senses, Mitch settled in the whirlpool beside her.

"So how about that mouth-to-mouth we were talking about?" He sat hip to hip beside her.

She slid over a few inches, inserting a little space between them. Playing games with Mitch was even more fun than she remembered. She didn't want it to be over too soon.

"You don't look like you need any rescuing."

His eyes took on a predatory gleam as he drifted closer. "I have the feeling *you're* going to need rescuing in a few more minutes."

Warmth pooled in her belly. The breathless play of bubbles over her skin became all the more sensual. Her breasts tingled, tightened.

"Really?"

He nodded. Underneath the water, his hands

reached for her waist, pulled her body into his lap. Water sluiced down her shoulders and over her chest. "Really. I've heard these are shark-infested waters."

His hands eased their way up her ribs to caress the undersides of her breasts. "And, honey, you look ripe for the eating." He leaned in to kiss the hollow at the base of her throat. His mouth burned a trail of fire down her chest to circle the crest of one taut nipple. "How can a man resist a bite?"

Gently, he drew her into her mouth, taking in as much flesh as he could for his private feast.

Tessa sighed and moaned and melted against him. She would definitely need rescuing if he kept this up. She felt as breathless as if she'd run a marathon.

He shifted his attention to her other breast while his hands surfed the landscape of her body beneath the water.

"You think we're slippery enough yet?"

She couldn't begin to answer that question. Not when he'd left her so hungry and wanting. She settled for an urgent wriggle in his lap, squeezing her chest to his.

"That's a yes." His answer sounded strangled.

He hauled her to her feet alongside him, then wrapped her in a towel. Together, they kissed, walked, stumbled their way to the bed sprawled in the middle of the living area.

"Are you ready for truth or dare, or have you had enough games for tonight?"

"I'm opting for truth," she responded, knowing it was her turn to be put in the hot seat. "Ask me anything."

Seized with a hunger for him she feared she

couldn't ever completely fill, Tessa pulled him down beside her and rained kisses over the wall of his chest. His wet skin held the scent of the utilitarian soap she'd used to make bubbles.

"I want to know what you are thinking about right now." His question mirrored hers at the bed-and-breakfast two nights ago.

"I'm thinking about how much I want to wrap my mouth around your—"

He covered her mouth with his palm. "Don't you dare say it, honey. I'm way too close already."

"I was prepared to tell the truth, Mitch." She'd really missed this game of theirs. "I think I win this round."

"You're the undisputed champ." He held his hands up in mock surrender.

She ventured a taste of him once her lips hit the flat plane of his abdomen. He groaned in time to the sweep of her tongue. His body stirred beneath her in immediate reaction.

She paused her tasting explorations to look at him. Ignoring his low growl of warning, she allowed her gaze to wander over him, taking in every gorgeous inch of Mitch Ryder. She might not fully understand his thrill-seeking ways or his need to wander and roam. But some part of her knew they belonged together in the most elemental way.

"Honey, you're killing me." Mitch's hoarse words drew her out of her reverie.

"I thought you wanted me to drive you wild." She rubbed her palm over his hip and brushed her cheek along the hot flesh of his waist.

The guttural sound that emerged from his throat was half curse and half plea.

"Consider it a job well done." He flipped her on her back to reverse their positions. His arms and chest made a tent around her, enclosing her completely. "But if you think it's not reciprocal, babe, you've just made a tactical error."

"I suppose you're going to make me sorry for that?" She loved the feeling of his big body around hers, overpowering her and protecting her at the same time.

"I'm going to make you very, very pleased." He lowered his abdomen and fanned a slow breath over her skin.

Chills broke out all over her. She shivered even as heat suffused her limbs.

The springs on the sofa bed squeaked as Mitch moved to one side of her, giving himself free reign over her body. She remained immobile, even with the weight of his body removed. The promise of his touch held her in thrall.

"Are you sure it's okay? I mean, with your knee and all?" She didn't want him to reinjure himself all over again just to prove a point of male pride.

"I can do this with one hand tied behind my back." Deliberately, he propped one hand under his head and let the other slide along her curves.

He could probably send her hurtling over the edge just by looking at her the right way, but Tessa kept that bit of information to herself. Instead, she closed her eyes and concentrated on the sweet slide of his hand on her belly as he dipped a finger beneath her damp panties.

"Tessa." He lingered over pink lace.

"Mmm?" She couldn't speak. Couldn't think.

"Tessa, open your eyes." His voice curled through her like steaming cocoa on a cold night. It heated her insides and warmed her to her toes.

She lifted her lids to look at him, but he didn't return her gaze. She followed his intent stare to the sight of his sun-tanned, masculine hand curled around her pale hip and the pink satin strings holding her panties together.

Captivated by the sight of his hand on her, Tessa twitched restlessly. She hated to admit defeat, but she needed more of him.

Soon.

"Please." Clamping her hands around his wrist, she forced him to cease his delicious torment. With gentle insistence, she guided his hand lower.

He obliged her by tugging the wet lace partially down her thighs. But he leaned close to whisper in her ear.

"So greedy, Tessa. When did my innocent little college coed grow so bold?" His fingers danced over her thighs, then slid her panties all the way off.

"I had a good teacher, remember?" She turned on her side to face him and wriggled against him with blatant wantonness.

"Remind me to thank that man." He withdrew a condom from the pocket of his discarded clothes.

Even as she hungered for him, a sense of satisfaction sang through her at the possessive way he looked at her, the urgent way he sheathed himself and drew her on top of him.

Surely he returned some of the feelings she had for

him. A man didn't want a woman that much without caring for her, too, did he?

When he pulled her mouth down to his and kissed her with an intensity that left her shaking, she thought no more about it. All that mattered at that moment was having Mitch inside her.

He fulfilled that wish in a heart-stopping stroke, filling her senses and her body.

"Oh!" She cried his name as the tension inside her built. The heat seemed unbearable when he massaged the most intimate folds of her flesh while they made love. "It's so good, Mitch." Her thoughts scattered as the coiling pressure teased and taunted her. "It's too much...I—"

Words fled when her climax crashed over her like a head-on collision. Her body tensed around him, drawing him along with her to a heady state of abandon.

For long moments, she could barely breathe. The force of her feelings for him scared her. She'd never felt so raw, so exposed to another person. Not even to him.

He pulled the covers over them and settled her beside him. In the falling twilight and fading firelight, they stared at each other like strangers over their first drink.

"Well..." he started.

"Yeah. Well."

"It was too much, wasn't it?" His eyes were wide and serious.

"You promised me it would be."

He remained still for a long moment, as if he had

forgotten his earlier boast. "Sometimes I don't know what the hell we're doing. Do you?"

She ventured a shaky smile, unsure how to break the tension that pervaded after an encounter that had been more intimate than just sex. "Nope."

"Let me hold you." He tucked her head against his chest and stroked her hair. "Maybe that will help."

As Tessa settled her cheek against his chest and absorbed the steady thump of his heart, however, she had the feeling his embrace wasn't going to help diffuse her growing feelings for him one bit.

MITCH STARED at the falling snow as he listened to the measured rise and fall of Tessa's breath. The winter blizzard unfolded in a white blur through the cabin window.

Outside, snow coated every twig and pine needle, casting the north country in a crystalline deep-freeze. Inside, he and Tessa had created a warm cocoon for themselves, wrapped in bleached thermal blankets and emotions that threatened to swamp him.

Had he fallen for her all over again? He sure as hell hadn't tried all that hard to resist her. But until now, he had thought he could handle it. He'd been sure he would either convince her to stay and help him market the business so they could continue to explore the incredible heat they generated whenever they were near one another. Or they would say goodbye after this week and move on with their lives.

Now, neither option pleased him.

After what had just passed between them, he didn't know if they could retreat to a mere sexual relationship. And he'd be damned if he'd let her leave again.

"You awake?" Her smoky voice wended through his thoughts.

"Yeah. I thought you were asleep." He resumed stroking her hair, idly freeing occasional silken tangles.

"No. Just thinking."

"I don't know, Tessa. If you're plotting more schemes to drive me wild, I might need some time to—"

"Not as young as you used to be, Casanova?" She grinned at him, her blond hair a halo in the light of the dying chemical log.

"In ten more minutes, you're going to pay for that one."

She laughed. The sound danced through him and around him, reminding him how happy they could make each other in some ways.

"Actually, I was thinking about business."

"Geez, Tessa. You're off the clock now. You can definitely think about other things." He'd rather hoped she was contemplating him or the fireworks they'd just generated.

"Not your business. I was thinking about my business."

"I thought they were inextricably linked this week." She'd spent every possible moment on his account. God knew the woman had given above and beyond the forty-hour workweek.

"That's my old business. Even though my plane doesn't leave until Sunday morning, technically, tomorrow is my last day on the job."

"But that's not the business you're thinking of, either?" His brain felt as frozen as the outside world. He couldn't seem to grasp her point.

"I'm thinking about my new business." She lifted her head from his chest and settled on the pillow beside him. Now they could look one another in the eye. "You remember. I mentioned that I had plans for life after Westwood Marketing."

"Your new business?"

"I'm officially going into business for myself as of next week, although I've been planning this venture for a long time."

"That's great." Then why did he feel like he'd been socked in the gut? He should be happy for her. "I'm sorry I haven't asked you more about it before now. Guess I've been too caught up in my own interests."

She shrugged off his apology. "I should have told you about it sooner. It still doesn't seem real to me."

It felt all too real to Mitch. She would be as committed to this new business as she had been to making a marketing career for herself eight years ago. That gave her plenty of incentive to leave him Sunday and not look back.

"What kind of company are we talking about?" he asked as an idea occurred to him. "If you're going to start your own marketing firm, I'd obviously transfer my business—"

"No, it's nothing like that." Her green gaze sparked with excitement. "I'm launching a line of women's career wear."

"Based in Miami."

Her brow furrowed. "Well, I guess it will be based in Miami because I'm there. But the neat thing about my concept is that it is completely virtual. There will be no storefront except on the Web."

"So no costly overhead and no employees until you're big enough to really support them."

"Right." She used one pink-fingernailed hand to clutch the blanket to her chest and the other to gesture as she grew more animated. "Except for a few telephone representatives, of course. But I've got a sort of unique concept for organizing the clothes by color palette or by type of business function a client needs to attend."

As she warmed to her topic and spoke enthusiastically about her future one thousand miles away from him, Mitch felt like someone had opened the front door of the cabin and ushered in the cold winds of the northeaster.

"I imagine your marketing know-how will ensure a successful launch." He wanted to sound supportive, but his words rang flat even in his own ears.

Her expression lost some of its fervor, and her grip on the white blanket tightened. "I hope so."

"You've got new territory to conquer now. A new business to perfect." He said it as much for his sake as for hers. The quicker he got the message that Tessa O'Neal was temporary, the better off they'd both be.

"Just like you," she observed, her chin tilting in defense. "It seems we're both undertaking new ventures."

"Just like last time. You're embarking on a new career, and I'm taking mine to the next level." With his words he drew a mental line in the sand, daring her to cross it or deny it.

In boardroom-barracuda style, she did neither. "So

it would seem." She couldn't have drawn her own line any more clearly.

They stared at one another across a pillow that seemed to stretch for miles. The room had grown dark except for the light of two utility candles Tessa had scrounged from a kitchen drawer. The soft flicker rimmed Tessa's hair with an angel's glow, softening his impression of her tough business facade.

"Does it intimidate you that I want to have a successful career?" Her voice was less defensive, more curious.

The question took him by surprise. "Hell, no. Why would you ask me a thing like that?"

"You obviously have no interest in my plans for the future. I guess I'm a little miffed about that." She glanced at her pink fingernails and seemed to make a point of relaxing her death grip on the thermal blanket. "Maybe even a little hurt."

He reached for her reflexively, forgetting all about his line in the sand. "It's not that I'm not interested." He regarded her steadily and tried not to notice how delectably soft she felt under his hands. "Believe me. I'd be interested in what you were doing even if we hadn't shared a bed—or a shower, in some cases—for the last two days. I'd want to hear all about your new business anyway because I think I could learn a hell of a lot just hearing how you've set the whole thing up. You've got a shrewd mind for this stuff."

"Thank you." She looked mildly placated, at best.

He must have hurt her more than he thought if she was still giving him the tilted chin. Damn. Even though he knew it was definitely not a good idea to get more tangled up with Tessa, he took hold of that stubborn chin and brought his lips down on hers.

She hesitated, a fraction of a second that let him know she'd been mad, before her mouth molded to his. The way it always had.

Like the first bite of cotton candy, or the lick of a new ice cream cone, she tasted soft and sweet. Except that when he kissed Tessa, he felt like he could go on forever.

Forever.

He scrambled back and broke contact, unwilling to let his mind travel down a path that wasn't meant to be for them. He struggled to remember why he'd given himself permission to kiss her in the first place.

Oh, yeah. He'd acted like a jerk.

"But more importantly, I want to know all about your business because it's yours."

"Then why did I get the cold shoulder when I mentioned it?" She sidled closer to him again, sneaking past his defenses and into his arms.

For a moment he considered racking his brain for a plausible lie. Why tell her the truth when he'd have to admit he'd practically fallen for her all over again?

But she deserved better than that.

"I guess it just hammered home to me that you're really leaving in a few days. I think I'd convinced myself I could still talk you into staying, somehow."

The green rims of her eyes were barely visible in the dim light of the cabin. Her wide, dark gaze studied him for a long moment, unnerving him.

"You really want me to stay?"

His pride warned him to keep his mouth shut. She'd rejected him the last time he'd tried to make her stay.

Besides, sooner or later his need to seek a thrill would drive her crazy.

Or really hurt her.

"You know I do." It pained him, but he managed a lopsided grin to lighten the moment. "I've done everything but offer to make you my vice president."

She blinked once. Twice. And then two more times in quick succession. "I guess I forgot about that." Her smoky voice rasped more than usual. "But Mogul Ryders will take off with or without me, Mitch. You've got a great product."

She couldn't have distanced herself more if she'd donned one of her battle-ready gray suits.

Clearly, she knew as well as he did that it was time to retreat. Their time together had been fun, but now they needed to face the reality that they weren't meant to be together.

Tessa had another business to perfect. And, in doing so, the farmer's daughter would put down even more roots in southern Florida.

As for Mitch, he still had the need to roam and the need to seek out the adrenaline highs that made life fun.

They still contrasted one another as much as they ever had. Mitch counted himself fortunate to remember that fact now, before he did something foolish.

Like fall the rest of the way in love with Tessa O'Neal.

12

As she stared out Mitch's truck window on the way to Lake Placid the next afternoon, Tessa tried to tell herself she was fortunate Mitch had pulled away from her. If he hadn't distanced himself from her last night, she might have done something stupid, like fall in love with him again.

Thank God she was smarter than that.

Mitch would only hurt her if she stuck around. She'd known that from the moment she'd set foot in Lake Placid. No matter how good he looked in ski pants, Mitch Ryder was all wrong for her.

He was the kind of guy who could up and leave at any time to promote his snowboards in the Alps or the Himalayas. And, lest her mushy heart forget, he was also a thrill-seeking maniac who liked to live on the edge. Who knew when he might decide to take up bungee jumping or skydiving?

She couldn't live like that—never knowing when he might take a risk that would rob him of what mobility he had left in his knee. Never knowing when he might really hurt himself. Or worse.

She closed her eyes to shove aside the distressing thoughts and quickly swiped the single tear that squeezed out. Ignoring the roar of a snowplow blowing by them and the incessant hum of the truck motor, Tessa tried to focus on her future and the business of her dreams.

A vision of her tidy home office where she would conduct the clothing company's daily affairs, however, failed to appear. Instead, she found herself dreaming about sitting in a toasty Adirondack log cabin, wrapped in an afghan while she worked at her computer.

For a moment, she allowed herself to enjoy the image. In her mind's eye, she saw Mitch wander through the picture to bring her a cup of cocoa. Dream Mitch set up his laptop next to hers and started his business day right beside her.

She opened her eyes, struck by the realization that she wasn't as smart as she thought she was.

Despite her best efforts to the contrary, she'd gone and fallen in love with Mitch all over again.

IF TESSA hadn't been feeling so miserable, she might have laughed at the way she and Mitch practically raced through the parking lot and up the steps to the Hearthside Inn. A few days ago they'd been hell-bent on getting out of the romantic hotel, the site of many old trysts.

Now that they'd been on the road together, they both knew that the sexual chemistry between them had nothing to do with *where* they were and everything to do with how *close* they were.

The Hearthside loomed like a home-free zone.

"I can manage from here on my own," Tessa offered as they reached the steps. She reached for her overnight bag, which he carried over one arm.

"Sorry, Tessa." He gestured toward the stairs and

bowed with a flourish. "My code of ethics demands I carry your bag."

"You could make an exception this once." She trudged up the stairs, weary from fighting her attraction to him. "Especially considering how eager you are to be rid of me."

"I'm eager to be rid of you?" He lowered his voice as he pushed open the front door for her. "I'm not the one who is counting the days until I leave Lake Placid in the dust—"

Mitch's words were drowned out by a feminine squeal from across the lobby.

"Hey, *chica!*"

Tessa watched Ines Cordova launch herself through the post-slopes ski crowd toward the front door. Even dressed in a chic ski jacket and boots, Ines bore her classic armor of bracelets and bangles. A brooch in the shape of a mantilla clipped a red wool scarf about her neck. She didn't look a minute older than Tessa, even though she was six years her senior.

"I have been so worried about you, I had to see you for myself." Ines hugged Tessa, enveloping her in a cloud of fragrant perfume.

"You traveled a thousand miles to check on me?" Last Tessa knew, she was one of Westwood's most competent account representatives. Surely Ines hadn't been all that worried.

"And how are you, Mitch?" Ines turned to give Mitch a hug, too. "It has been a long time, no?"

Tessa swallowed the urge to yank her gorgeous best friend out of his arms. After all, Ines and Mitch had developed a friendship during the week they'd all spent in Lake Placid. Mitch and Ines seemed like kindred free spirits compared to Tessa.

"Eight years," Mitch clarified, taking a small step back. "You haven't changed a bit."

Ines laughed and winked. "Maybe I haven't tried hard enough. In fact I was just explaining to my friend J.D. that I...now where did he get off to?"

"J.D.?" Tessa and Mitch spoke together as one voice.

Ines craned her neck to scan the hotel lobby. "Oh, there he is." She waved her arm, causing the bracelets around her wrist to jangle a musical tune. "Over here, J.D.!"

Tessa watched as J.D. Drollette, the Voice of the Adirondacks, lumbered to his feet from one of the lobby's rocking chairs. He rose like a mountain among the other hotel guests.

She heard Mitch mutter something under his breath, but she couldn't be sure what. She did notice he finally set down her overnight bag. Seeing J.D. must have made him realize he wasn't going to escape this conversation, or her, anytime soon.

"Hello, there, my friends." J.D. extended his hand to Tessa and Mitch. He looked marginally neater than the last time she saw him, but his jacket still bore the rumpled look of a forty-year-old bachelor who didn't believe in dry cleaning. He couldn't have contrasted more with Ines's polished presentation if he'd tried. "Ines and I have been worried about you two."

"I tried your cell phone all night," Ines interjected. "But J.D. said that the cells don't always go through in the mountains, even in the best of weather."

"Did you find a place to stay?" J.D. asked.

This was worse than coming home late as a teenager. Ines and J.D. did a perfect imitation of fretful parents.

Thankfully, Mitch stepped in. "We found a place to stay at Buck Pond. The ranger let us take one of the cabins because the weather was so bad. I'm surprised you could even manage to travel, Ines."

Tessa applauded his smooth redirection of the conversation.

"I flew into Albany and drove up from there," Ines explained, as if that answered everything.

"Roads were dry as a bone south of here," J.D. added, flashing a friendly grin in Ines's direction. "The storm really only hit the northern Adirondacks and then it moved east."

"We watched the weather station on television, and those graphic snowflakes were centered right over the two of you on their map," Ines offered, winking as if the snow had been some sort of divine providence.

"No surprise there," Tessa muttered. The fates seemed to be conspiring against her, driving her toward Mitch no matter how desperately she fought a relationship with him.

Mitch leaped on the lull in the conversation and turned to Tessa. "Well, now that Ines is here for you to visit with, I guess I'll head back home."

Ines started to object, her jewelry clanking a discordant note.

J.D. slung a heavy arm around Ines's shoulders and quieted the jangling. "Why don't you ride back to the mountain with me?" He spoke in slow, deliberate tones, more effective than Ines's rush of words. "The sno-cross events are finishing up in an hour or so and we can grab a couple of beers at the after party."

Tessa would definitely ask Ines how she got to be such fast friends with J.D.

In the meantime, she noticed Mitch fidget. It was obvious he'd sooner break his leg again then go face his old snow-hound cronies.

"Aren't you commentating this week, J.D.?" Mitch deftly changed the subject. "I'm surprised you're not at the sno-cross finals."

J.D. shrugged. "I pick and choose what I want to commentate. There aren't any local kids in the event that my listeners will want to follow." He quirked an eyebrow in Mitch's direction. "So how about that beer?"

Mitch started to back away. "Sorry, J.D., I'll catch you another time. Tessa and I need to go over some more business before she jets out of here this weekend." He sent Tessa a steady look. "What do you say, Tessa? I'll meet you back here at seven?"

He must really not want to go anywhere near the event on the mountain if he was willing to spend more time with her. Hadn't he been eager to part company only an hour ago?

"Seven is fine," she agreed. They did have business to finish up, after all. Besides, she had come to Lake Placid to face her past and put it behind her.

She wouldn't be able to do that if she hid from Mitch.

Mitch waved as he pushed through the hotel's front door. A draft blew in behind him, a gust of cold air that left Tessa shivering at his departure.

"Come on, *chica*." Ines locked arms with her. "We will go to your room and talk."

Tessa was too wrung out from the last few days to argue. She let Ines lead her toward the elevator.

"Wait." Tessa turned to retrieve her luggage. "I need my bag."

Ines held her fast. "J.D. will get it."

"Geez, Ines, he hardly knows me." She tugged her arm free from her friend. "He's certainly not going to know which bag—"

Ines reeled her toward the elevator as the muted bell signaled its arrival. "Of course he will. I nodded at it as we left."

"Oh. Excuse me. I didn't know you nodded." Tessa allowed the sarcasm to hang from her words. She shook her head as she let Ines pull her onto the elevator. "What is going on with you two, Ines? And what in God's name are you doing in Lake Placid, anyway?"

"I am here to help." She frowned at Tessa and then smoothly punched the number for the executive suite. "It is obviously a good thing I got here when I did."

"You know my room number?" Tessa knew she sounded miserable and grouchy, but then again, she felt miserable and grouchy. What depressed her most was knowing that she'd feel ten times worse once she left Lake Placid and would never see Mitch again.

"*Si*, Tessa! J.D. and I have been waiting for you all day. The first thing I did when I got here was confirm your room number." She sighed as she stepped off the elevator on the third floor. "Besides, I have your travel file with me. All I had to do was look it up in the Westwood records."

"But what are you doing here in the first place?" Tessa struggled for patience with Ines as she jammed the electronic key into the slot. Ines had always been a brilliant marketing strategist and a skillful manager, but she could be the world's most annoying friend when she decided to interfere in Tessa's personal life.

"I told you, I came to help." Ines brushed by her into the room, moving straight toward the phone and dialing room service while J.D. silently brought in Tessa's bag.

"You want some dinner?"

Twenty minutes later, Tessa was showered and changed and seated before a plate of broiled trout. The world seemed marginally better now that she could eat. The oranges and cinnamon bread that had been her diet since last night left her with a ravenous appetite.

"Okay, 'fess up, Ines. You've stalled long enough. I want to know what you are doing here."

Ines idly stirred a pink frothy concoction she'd ordered from the bar. "Well, I'd hoped I was coming here for a wedding, but it seems you are not progressing so well on your own in the matrimonial department."

Tessa would have squawked if she didn't have a mouth full of trout. She settled for making a bug-eyed face.

"Don't look so surprised, Tessa. You must know I had high hopes you would iron things out with Mitch once I strong-armed you into taking this assignment."

"Iron things out? Ines, we ironed things out a long time ago." She pulled the pink drink from Ines's hand and set it on the table with a slosh.

"So why are you sleeping with him again?" Ines snatched her glass and shot Tessa a mutinous expression. Her dangling parrot earrings shimmied in response.

"You—" Tessa shook her finger in mute anger.

"I am a brazen bitch, I know." Ines flashed her a cheeky grin and sipped her bubble-gum colored brew. "But I call it like I see it, honey, and you have it for this man. Big-time."

Deflated, Tessa slumped in her chair. "We want each other, but other than that, we don't want any of the same things."

"He's got a business of his own now, and so do you. How is that so different?"

Tessa shook her head. "He seems to pull away from me whenever I talk about the new business."

"Maybe he's intimidated by your success." Ines shelved her drink, warming up to a discussion of her favorite topic.

Men.

"I know that's not it. He can't tell me enough what a great job I'm doing with Mogul Ryders."

"Then maybe he's just reacting to the fact that you're starting a business a thousand miles away from him." She folded her arms and lifted her eyebrows in an I-told-you-so look. "If he had any hopes that you would stick around, that would have squashed them in a New York minute."

Could it be true? Despite Ines's tendency to be a little overbearing with her mothering ways, she did know a thing or two about men.

"You think *he* wants *me* to stick around? He's the

one who's always had a hard time staying in one place."

"Not anymore. Look around you! He owns the hotel. He's making snowboards." She winked at Tessa. "And I learned from the receptionist that he's even built his own house. Doesn't that mean he's staying in one place?"

Mitch putting down roots?

"I guess all signs point to yes." It seemed hard to believe, knowing what a thrill-seeker he'd always been. "But if he wanted me to stick around as anything more than his personal promoter, why hasn't he said as much?"

Ines leaned forward in her seat. "If you were receptive to staying, why didn't *you* tell *him* as much?"

"Well..."

"Men do not know unless we tell them, *chica*. Men don't even know their own hearts unless we help them figure it out. You've come all this way, but from where I'm sitting, I don't see that you've ventured anything."

The idea haunted Tessa even after Ines had finally jingled her way down the hall to seek her own room.

Was it possible Mitch didn't know how she felt about him? Would he be so quick to say goodbye if he knew her feelings ran even deeper than the last time she'd fallen in love with him? Her eight years of life experience gave her a greater appreciation for Mitch. She'd learned the hard way that what they had together didn't happen every day.

Maybe if she put her heart on the line this time, something she hadn't truly done eight years ago, maybe things would be different between them.

Resolved to try, Tessa shed her stuffy business suit and searched for the perfect ensemble to wear for the most important meeting of her life.

"YOU LOOK LIKE HELL, old man," pro shop manager Shawn Dougall announced when he showed up uninvited on Mitch's front doorstep.

Mitch squinted through the megawatts reflecting off Shawn's fluorescent green jacket. "You're not exactly winning any fashion awards in that get-up, either."

"Can I come in, at least?" Not waiting for an answer, he shoved by Mitch and sauntered into the cabin. He whistled between his teeth as he looked around. "This place looks great. Have you been fixing it up?"

"I needed more room," Mitch explained, sinking back into the recliner he'd occupied ever since he got home from his trip with Tessa. He followed Shawn's gaze to the newest addition on his house.

Two weeks ago he'd knocked out the back wall to add a den with a big picture window overlooking the mountain. Mitch had forgotten to tell Shawn about his recent renovations. Tessa seemed to keep his mind off everything but her hot body and sharp mind this week. And not always in that order.

Shawn wiped his boots, then found a seat on the couch. He reached for the remote and flipped on the big screen television. Finding a hoop game, he muted the sound and sighed. "Man, you've got it made with this setup."

Mitch could hardly remember when life had been so simple that a cool house and satellite television seemed like the answer to his problems. He closed his eyes and settled deeper into the recliner. "I guess."

"What do you mean, I guess?" Shawn zapped the TV into a tiny white dot on the screen before it faded to black. "You've got a legendary reputation on the slopes. You made enough money to live off your interest. You're living in freaking paradise here, and to top it all off, a sexy beach babe shows up and wants to run away with you for three days." Shawn shook his head. "You really are an old man if that doesn't make you happy."

Mitch lifted in a lazy eyelid. "Tessa? A beach babe?"

Shawn shrugged his shoulders. "What else do you call a long-legged blond with a Florida tan and freckles on her nose?"

"Don't be checking out her nose, man." When the hell had Shawn gotten close enough to notice her freckles? Not that Tessa would pay any mind to a college kid. Would she? "She's not available."

"No?"

"She's mine." Mitch couldn't stop the thought before it fell from his lips.

"Like everything else," Shawn muttered.

"What?" Mitch straightened in his recliner, wrenching the lever for the footrest to put his feet on the floor.

"You heard me." Shawn pitched the remote from hand to hand. "You've got a lock on everything around here. It's bad enough you hold all the snowboard titles and all the records. Now you've also got to take the most gorgeous woman to descend on Lake Placid in a long time and turn yourself into some business mogul, too. It could make some guys—you

know, guys without an ego as resilient as mine—a little jealous."

Mitch stared at him, shocked that their usual kid-
ding around had taken a sobering twist.

Shawn flicked the TV on and surfed a dozen sports
channels. "You gonna ask me how I did this week?"

At that moment, Shawn's perplexing speech made
perfect sense. Mitch had been a quasi-coach to his
snowboarding friend, and he hadn't even bothered to
find out how Shawn fared in the recent competition.

"I'm sorry—"

"Don't be sorry, man. Just ask me how I did."

"How'd you do?"

"Third place in the big air competition and first
place in the superpipe event."

"First?" Mitch jumped out of his chair. The twinge
in his knee reminded him why he could no longer be a
contender.

Shawn couldn't suppress a laugh. Mitch punched
him in the arm.

"You came in first?" Mitch hadn't felt so proud
since he'd won his own first meet. "I should've seen
it."

"It's no big deal." Shawn rose and tossed the remote on the couch. "Daniela brought Joey to see the
meet," he added, referring to the Hearthside maid and
her ten-year-old son. "The kid followed me around
like a shadow. Sort of like me and you all over again."

"I should have been there, too." Mitch remembered
how disappointing it had been that his father never
bothered to come to any of his games. As far as Mitch
knew, he was the closest thing to family Shawn had. A
pang of guilt pinched him more than his old knee in-

jury. "Besides, I want to be there to take some credit for your success."

"Yeah?"

"Definitely."

"Righteous." He ambled toward the front door but paused before leaving. "You know I was just giving you a hard time before about you having a lock on everything, right?"

"Of course." Mitch knew Shawn had been dead serious, but he wasn't about to begrudge the man an opportunity to speak his mind. "I obviously didn't walk away with a first and a third place today. That's all you."

"You would have taken first in everything." Shawn laughed as he tromped down the front steps. "But I'm happy with what I've got."

And that's exactly why Shawn was such an easy guy to hang out with, Mitch thought as he wandered inside. Shawn didn't obsess about taking first place, the way Mitch always had.

Their conversation had shaken Mitch's world more than he cared to admit. Shawn's mild observations put a few cracks in the mirror of Mitch's self-perception— a mirror long tainted by his father's demanding views.

For too long, Mitch had single-mindedly pursued whatever he'd wanted. His determination had earned him countless first place prizes on the mountain, a legendary reputation and a business that would no doubt keep him well stocked in troll pins into the next millennium.

What it hadn't earned him was Tessa. He had tried to keep her tied to him eight years ago by asking her to tour the world on the international snowboard circuit, but it hadn't worked. He wouldn't be fool enough to try forcing her to stick around now.

Sure, he'd put down a few roots of his own, something he hadn't even realized he'd been doing until she'd shown up. He had ties to the community and he had a commitment to his business—things that could make Tessa happy.

But he also had the sense he could walk away from it all tomorrow if the mood struck. What if another opportunity came along? A chance to be in the spotlight? A thrill too enticing to pass up?

How could he be certain he wouldn't walk away from her and hurt her all over again?

That was one risk he was unwilling to take.

13

WHEN MITCH walked into the Hearthside's deserted library that night, he wished like hell he *was* ready to take that risk.

Tessa stood with her back to him, staring out the window at the light fall of snow and wearing a tangerine-colored dress with about as much skirt as a French maid's outfit.

"That's quite a dress," he managed between deep, stabilizing breaths.

That, of course, was one hell of an understatement.

She looked like a screen siren from some sex-drenched B movie. Her hair fell in loose waves to the middle of her back. Her outfit had little see-through holes everywhere, like the tablecloths his grandma used to knit. As much as he squinted, however, it seems she had strategically covered up the most intriguing parts with what little dress she had.

"Thank you." She turned and sauntered toward him. Only then did he notice the strappy high heels that accentuated her tiny ankles and long legs.

"No. Thank you." He openly gawked at her, but he really had no choice. His business agenda forgotten, he could only think about covering her with his body and peeling that come-hither get-up off of her. "I've never seen you look so..."

"Slinky?" She stopped just in front of him and smiled.

If they hadn't been in a public place where someone could walk in anytime, Mitch would have kissed her breathless and cruised every curve of her body with his hands.

But he knew if he allowed himself to do those things, there would be no stopping.

"Gorgeous."

Tessa congratulated herself on attracting his attention. She had it in spades. In fact, she had done so well that she wasn't sure she would be able to divert his attention from the dress to listen to what she had to say.

And she had come here with a greater purpose than simply getting him to look at her as more than a business associate.

"We need to talk," she announced, gently lifting his chin to encourage his gaze.

He smiled the slow, sexy grin that had always made her heart skip a beat. "Honey, I was just thinking that no words are needed at times like this."

He started to reach for her, but Tessa stepped back. If he touched her now, they'd only wind up in bed again, and they'd never get anything resolved between them. If she was going to tell him how she felt, she had to do it now, before it was too late.

"Let's sit." She walked toward the big couch, but Mitch's hands settled on her hips and steered her toward the smaller love seat.

Not *their* love seat, but a sofa just as intimate.

She found herself ensconced in the private nook at the far end of the room, hidden from view of the entryway by a massive grandfather clock.

"But we really do need to talk." She scooted to the far side of seat and glared at Mitch until he gave her some room.

He closed his eyes for a long moment. When he opened them, the hungry look had abated a little bit. "The next time you want to talk, Tessa, I suggest you rethink your wardrobe."

"I thought out my wardrobe very carefully," she admonished. "I even went so far as to check out my own Web site to be sure I chose the right kind of outfit for this occasion."

"What kind of occasion is this?"

"Well, I found this dress listed under the man-killer category."

Mitch groaned. "Aptly titled. Next time choose something from the make-man-listen category. You need something with less holes and more skirt."

"The things in that category are all navy blue, and I know how you feel about that." Tessa smoothed her fingers over the skirt of her crocheted dress. "I wanted to be sure I got your attention tonight—"

"Mission accomplished."

"—because I'm making a play for you."

"What?" He went very still.

"You heard me."

"I'm sure I misunderstood. Could you repeat it?"

Did he have to make this harder for her? She'd never pursued a man in her life. Now, in the course of one week, she'd seduced Mitch and was in the process of asking him to consider some kind of commitment. The insistent tick of the grandfather clock made her all the more aware of her dwindling time in Lake Placid.

"I want us to be together." There. She'd said it.

In a blink, he was across the love seat and pulling her into his lap.

"I want that, too." The proof of his statement pressed into her thigh.

A beam of heat streaked through her. She had sorely mismanaged this meeting.

"I mean in more ways than that," she clarified, pushing against his chest to insert some space between them. "I want us to be together beyond Sunday."

"You mean it?" An expression she'd never seen before animated his features, but she recognized the tone in his voice.

Hope.

"Yes." She'd gone long enough telling herself she could get along without him. Now, all that seemed to matter was working out the differences between them.

"But what about your business?" No longer focused on her dress, Mitch's gaze bored directly into hers. He squeezed her shoulders, as if he could will from her the answers he wanted to hear.

"I've let business run me long enough. *I'm* going to run this business." The words felt so right. So true. The flexibility was what made an Internet business so appealing in the first place. "And I'm going to do it from wherever I happen to be at the time, whether it's propped up in bed working on my laptop or making phone calls from a desk in the Adirondacks."

"You want to stay." The words whispered across the small space between them. His grip eased until his hands stroked down her arms with infinite tenderness. "You want to be with me."

"Yes..." Of course she'd also hoped that he would put himself on the line to a certain extent. If she were willing to forsake her roots, to become a wanderer with him, would he curb his thrill-seeking ways just a little?

"But what?" His expression clouded.

She climbed off his lap and sat beside him again. "But nothing. I definitely want to be with you, Mitch. I made a mistake when I married my husband because I wasn't really over you. I don't want to go on to make more mistakes because I didn't have the courage to try and work things out between us."

"Right." He nodded, his gaze still wary. "So far that all sounds good, but I have the sense that I'm waiting for the other ski boot to drop."

Tessa rushed out the rest before she lost her nerve. "All I want is for you to have some courage, too. I mean, I guess if I'm going to reorganize my life to move cross-country to be with you, I'm kind of hoping you might be willing to bend a little and meet me half-way."

He stared at her, uncomprehending. "You mean like Virginia?"

"No, Mitch! Like—"

"I know, honey." He gathered her hands and kissed them. "It was a bad joke."

"Then you know what I'm getting at?"

"You're asking me to change."

"Well, no. Not exactly." She knew better than to change a man, didn't she?

"You expect me to be a different man than I am." All traces of humor vanished from his face.

For the first time, Tessa realized how often he hid

his feelings with a joke. He'd been less intimidating with the perpetual grin. Now, as he assessed her with fathomless gray eyes, she understood that there was much more to him than he let the world see.

"No." She prayed she comprehended him as well as she thought she did. "I'm gambling that you're a different man than the Mitch I met eight years ago. You're a business owner, a staple in the community here. You must be ready to put down some roots here now. Right?"

Time ticked by on the old grandfather clock in the corner of the room. Every soft swish of the pendulum eroded a little more of her hope for the future.

"You didn't want me the first time around, but you'd take me now if I can promise I'm not the man I used to be?" His voice was devoid of the vibrance she normally associated with him.

"That's not exactly accurate. I—"

"Hell, that shouldn't be too hard, should it?" He shook his head, a wry smile on his face. "We both know my knee prohibits me from pursuing the career you objected to last time. That alone ought to help me pass your test. I mean, how many thrills can I seek with a bum leg?"

Tessa had envisioned countless scenarios in which Mitch rejected her overture tonight, but she hadn't once imagined his laughing facade hid this bitterness.

"I don't know, Mitch. Your physical limitation doesn't matter to me. How you deal with it does. If you are going to continue to run high-stakes risks for the rest of your life just to prove to yourself you can still do it, then we don't have anything more to say to one another."

A part of her couldn't believe she sat here fighting for him after all this time. Yet this was the kind of talk she'd had with him in her dreams, the kind of conversation they hadn't been ready to have eight years ago.

She reached for his hand and held it between hers. She stroked the corded area between his knuckles and his wrist, memorizing the way the veins networked across his flesh. Would she ever know another man of such vitality?

"But if you think you are finished taking crazy chances," she continued, "and if you think you are done risking your life just to snag an adrenaline high and maybe prove something to your dad while you're at it—"

He laid a gentle finger over her lips. "My old man has nothing to do with the risks I take."

"Sorry. I just wanted to point out that if you think you've moved beyond that stage of your life, I would really like to see if we can get along for more than a week."

"We've never tried, have we?" He smoothed her hair from temple to shoulder, then lifted a handful to his cheek and scrubbed it against his stubbled jaw. "It's amazing how well I know you when we've only been together for a sum total of three weeks in our lives."

"You don't know that much about me." She argued the point for the hell of it. Or maybe to stall. She would put off his rejection for as long as possible, because she didn't know how she would ever face it.

"I know you like AM radio because I hear you singing snatches of stuff like 'California Dreaming' and 'Happy Together' that most hip millennium women wouldn't be caught dead listening to. The fact that you drag your father's oranges to the ends of the earth tells me you were a bit of a daddy's girl."

She felt a grin tug at her lips, which was a miracle considering how depressed she felt, knowing he would opt to set her free forever. He was right on both counts, but she wasn't about to tell him that.

"You value time more than money, but you give away both to help other people. Your biggest weakness as a businessperson is you don't know how to cut people off when they are talking, and you'll listen to anyone who needs you."

This hit closer to home. How did he know that?

"Of course," he continued, undaunted, "this is also one of your key strengths as a marketer because you listen better than anyone I've ever met. You have the unique ability to know just how to please your clients, a talent that probably surprises other people but is a simple result of how much you pay attention to what you hear."

She fidgeted in her chair. His words practically mirrored the verbiage of the exit evaluation Ines had given her two weeks ago. Maybe Ines had talked to him about her.

"You've also got a white cat, a mild addiction to caffeine and six freckles on your nose."

"Aha!" She pressed a finger to his chest in triumph. "I got rid of my cat six weeks ago." She allowed herself a superior grin. For a moment. "How did you know about the cat?"

Mitch watched her smile slide away. He loved Tessa's expressiveness. In fact, as he sat there thinking through all he knew about Tessa, he realized he loved everything about her. "One of your gray suits had a couple of cat hairs on the skirt."

"Ugh!" She strove to make sure that never happened. "My dry cleaner is fired."

He listened to the clock tick, saying nothing as she chattered about his supposed great knowledge about her. Of course, he hadn't begun to enumerate all the little things he knew about her. He'd pushed away thoughts of her for eight years, but he gave into them now, knowing they wouldn't be together again after tonight.

One of his favorite things about Tessa was her uncanny ability to get close to people. She had a way of making strangers feel like they knew her after only a few minutes of conversation. That's how he'd felt when he met her.

How he'd felt ever since.

It had taken him ten minutes to fall snowboard over ass in love with her eight years ago. And now that she was finally returning his feelings and ready to do something about them, he had wised up enough to realize why they couldn't be together.

His timing really sucked.

But he'd be damned if he'd hurt her.

"The dress isn't working, is it?" Her comment startled him out of his thoughts.

"You slayed me the moment I walked in here." He tried to give her the grin he knew would set her at ease, but he couldn't seem to call it up. "The mankiller apparel definitely works."

"That's why you're paying more attention to the grandfather clock than me." She stood, then paced about with restless energy.

Their time had run out. He wasn't ready for it, but he knew the honorable thing to do.

"I'm sorry, honey." He rose from the love seat, too, then planted himself in her pacing path. He pulled each of her hands into one of his own and held them tight. "I was just thinking about how well I know you, sort of taking off on a mental tangent after our conversation."

She searched his eyes, seeking answers he couldn't give. Mitch felt a weight descend on him.

"You're going to tell me to take the first flight back to Miami, aren't you?" Her green gaze narrowed. A tiny thread of anxiety wound through her voice.

He shook his head, unable to deny it with words. "I was going to tell you that I also know you well enough to know you could never be happy with me."

"Why don't you let me decide that?" She squeezed his hands.

"Even if you were happy to move around with me and run your business via laptop, that doesn't address the more basic problem between us."

She bit her lip. That gesture, so self-conscious and worried, so utterly unlike Tessa, made him feel like a heel.

"You won't quit the breakneck pursuit of the next thrill?" She obviously knew it as well as he did.

"I don't know that I can."

She started to interrupt, no doubt to offer a solution of some sort, but he covered her lips with the pad of his thumb. The softness of her mouth reminded him of one more thing he would miss about her.

"Tessa, I could tell you right now that I would try my damnedest. But I've never been the type of guy to sit on the sidelines of life and watch everyone else have fun. I don't know that I could to it."

She wrenched his hand away from her mouth. "I'm not asking for a guarantee. I just wanted some assurance that you'd try." She cupped his jaw in her palm, grazing her fingertips over his cheek. "Why can't you try?"

"Because you deserve a guarantee, damn it, and I want that guarantee for you. I want to know that your next husband isn't ever going to hurt you like your first." The idea that she would go on to wed someone else scraped his raw nerves. "You deserve forever."

Her hand slid from his cheek.

"And you can't give me that?" Her words were soft, but her voice didn't waver, her tone didn't plead.

"Not when I know I might disappoint you. Not when there's still any chance I could cave to the enticement of the next mountain."

"I see." She took two steps back. "Then maybe we'd better move on to business so we can sew up this project and I can be on my way."

"That's okay." He couldn't bear to sit beside her and not hold her. He'd forget all his stupid nobility and spirit her away to his house to spend the week in bed. "I've realized I'm probably going to have to find a full-time, dedicated marketing director."

"That would be wise." She tucked a stray blond hair behind her ear. In spite of the screen-siren dress, Tessa had never looked more distant. "I can oversee the Web site development for you until you get someone else."

"No. You need to think about your own business

now. You've spent more than enough time helping me with mine."

"Then, if it's okay with you, I think I'll just see about switching my flight to tomorrow." She gave him a halfhearted smile. "No sense sticking around here to make this any more painful."

Was it his imagination, or did the ticking of the grandfather clock grow louder? The library remained still and silent except for that incessant tick.

"I understand."

She retrieved a tiny orange purse from a curio table near the window. "Then I guess I'll say good-night." She strode forward and stuck out her hand, as if they were closing a business meeting.

He wanted to pull her into his arms, not shake her hand. But he wouldn't rob her of her dignity. He took her hand and brought it to his lips for a restrained kiss.

Still, in spite of his best efforts, he found himself lingering over the softness of her citrus-scented skin.

Abruptly, she reclaimed her hand. "Goodbye, Mitch."

And without so much as a glance backward, she sailed out of the door and out of his life.

Again.

"LET ME get this straight." Ines sat on Tessa's bed the next morning, watching Tessa pack. "You put your heart on the line and told him you were in love with him, yet he said he was not willing to try?"

Tessa crammed her silk blouses in her suitcase, heedless of wrinkles. She didn't care if she ever wore anything from this trip again. "I didn't put it in those words, exactly."

"You didn't tell him you love him?"

"He knows." She pulled the tangerine dress out of the closet. "You need a sexy dress?"

Ines held up one of the long crocheted sleeves. "Ooh, la la, *chica!* The man must be made of stone if he could see you in this and not snap you up."

A vivid memory of her sitting on Mitch's lap last night stole through Tessa's mind. God knows he'd felt hard as a rock when she'd pressed against him.

"Maybe he is." She thrust the dress into Ines's arms. "All I know is it didn't work for me, so it's all yours."

Ines eyed it appreciatively. "This may be just the thing I need to open J.D.'s eyes."

"J.D.?" Tessa zipped her cosmetics bag and stuffed it into her suitcase. "You really have your sights set on J.D. Drollette?"

"And why not?" Ines grinned. "It gives me shivers just to stand next to him. I've never felt so safe and so sexy at the same time."

Tessa could see them together. J.D. might lose that longtime rumpled bachelor look, and Ines might finally ditch some of the jeweled armor she used to keep the rest of the world at a distance. It could work.

"I'm glad for you," Tessa murmured, hoping her friend would have better luck with men than she did. "You're going to stay for a little while then?"

"*Si.* I had hoped to be here for a wedding." She withdrew a scrap of blue satin from a piece of tissue paper in her purse. "Remember?"

A garter.

"I remember." Tessa slammed the lid of her suitcase closed. "Very presumptuous of you."

"Maybe not." Ines twirled the delicate blue garter

around her finger. "Your flight doesn't leave until this afternoon."

"I won't even see Mitch again, Ines." Normally, Tessa didn't mind her friend's eternal romanticism. But this morning, knowing things were over between her and Mitch, it hurt like hell. "Besides, I've got to get the rental car back and drive two hours to the airport. I'll probably head out soon."

The garter stopped twirling. "Oh, no, Tessa, you've got to stay a little longer than that. Give Mitch time to come to his senses."

"Apparently he's already come to them and realized what a bad idea we are together." Tessa yanked her suitcase off the bed and headed for the door of her suite. She was almost there when she spied the lemon yellow ski coat on the couch. "Damn. You need a coat, Ines?"

"Is it new?" Ines asked. At Tessa's nod, Ines bundled it into a hotel laundry bag. "Then let us try to return it. It cost too much money for you to just give it away."

"That's okay." Tessa reached for the doorknob. "You can use it while you're up here."

Ines scrambled to insert herself between the door and Tessa. "You really can't leave just yet."

"Why not?" The sooner the better, as far as Tessa was concerned.

"J.D. said Mitch went out to the mountain this morning." Ines took Tessa's suitcase and set it on the floor.

"So?"

"So, maybe Mitch is making a last-ditch effort to come to terms with himself."

"Or maybe he's practicing his spins now that I'm not around to pitch a fit about it."

"Well, do me a favor and help me return your jacket before you go, just in case Mitch comes flying back here to tell you how wrong he's been."

"Ines—"

"I'm still your boss today, *chica*. Don't make me have to pull rank on you." Ines passed the laundry bag full of yellow parka to Tessa.

"Fine." Tessa took the bag in one arm and grabbed Ines by the other. "But after this, I'm out of here."

After they returned the coat, Tessa wouldn't be able to make tracks fast enough.

Knowing Mitch had definitely taught her how to say goodbye.

14

Mitch tugged the zipper of his ski jacket up in an effort to keep out the wind whipping off Whiteface Mountain. Too bad it didn't come close to keeping the chill out of his heart.

He stood at the base of the mountain and stared at the three thousand feet of snow and rock that had challenged, rewarded and sometimes frustrated him throughout his snowboarding career. He'd been down every trail in one way or another. He'd ridden on snowboards, skis, sleds, sno-cross bikes and—all too frequently—his butt.

It had been nearly two years since he'd taken the chairlift all the way to the top. Not since his accident overseas. He'd come out here to help Shawn prep for competition and to see how much activity he could handle after his knee injury. On those occasions he'd been careful to only go about halfway up the mountain.

"Hey, Mitch!" A voice carried on the wind behind him.

Too bad the sound was a gruff baritone instead of Tessa's throaty alto. He turned to see J.D. stomping through the snow.

Mitch raised a hand in greeting. "I didn't expect to see you still in town this morning."

J.D. shrugged. "I've got some vacation time coming. I thought I'd stick around Lake Placid for a few days."

"Finally treating yourself to a little fun?"

J.D. seemed to work nonstop covering events around the north country.

"Treating myself to a few dates with Ines Cordova." J.D. grinned like a man who's just discovered a winning lottery ticket.

"Good for you." Mitch hoped J.D. would have more success working things out with a Florida marketing maven than he'd had. "I take it Ines is going to be sticking around here a little longer?"

"Another week, at least." J.D. cupped his hands together and breathed into them to warm them up. "I hear Tessa is flying out today, though."

Mitch nodded. She'd left a message for him at the front desk, along with some of her files on Mogul Ryders. He hadn't been able to think about her leaving. Instead, he'd focused all his energy on getting out to Whiteface today and confronting his reluctance to take part in his former world.

"Ines thought you two had something going on between you."

Understatement of the year.

He and Tessa had nearly burned the Hearthside down last night with the heat that sizzled between them just from being in the same room together. There was definitely something going on between them, but Mitch hadn't been able to assure her he wouldn't screw it up.

"Not anymore," Mitch finally answered. God, he hated that answer.

"You want to talk about it?" J.D. prodded, easily

slipping into the mentor role he'd long ago adopted with Mitch.

"Nah. I want to get to the top of the mountain. You want to come?" He couldn't think about Tessa right now. His emotions were still too raw to take them out and examine them in the cold mountain air.

"Sure." J.D. practically marched toward the chairlift lines, his snowboard in hand. "I wondered if you were ever going to face this thing again."

Mitch walked more slowly, resigned to his decision but unsure what he would do once he got up there.

"Where's your board?" J.D. asked as they started to take their seats on the lift.

"Don't need it."

J.D. shook his head. "That accident must have spooked you more than you let on to the media."

"Not really." Mitch perched on the far side of the chairlift to help balance J.D.'s six-foot-nine-inch frame.

"No?" J.D. eased the safety bar over them. "Then why are you afraid to board down Whiteface?"

"You've got it all wrong." Mitch wished it were that simple. Hell, if he were afraid to take risks, he and Tessa wouldn't have a major obstacle between them right now. He could live life on the sidelines so she wouldn't continually fear for him.

"You don't need to be ashamed of being afraid—"

"I'm not ashamed, man." Mitch looked down at the tops of the pine trees as the lift took them higher and tried not to think about how much this ride used to exhilarate him. "I *am* scared. But not of boarding down Whiteface. I'm scared of going back to the top of the mountain and feeling that one-of-a-kind, on top of the world feeling that you can only get from being at the summit. For nearly two years I've avoided the mountaintop like a plague because I couldn't stand getting up there and knowing I wouldn't ever have a kick-butt ride down again."

The air got thinner, colder, as they went upward. Mitch looked at the mountain, remembering other times he had sat here, plotting his strategy for his next run.

The top of the mountain would never give him the same high it did back then.

"Let me get this straight." J.D. rubbed his jaw. "You're telling me you're not afraid to go down the mountain, just to be at the top."

"You got it."

"And that's because you know that no ride down will ever be the same because of your knee." J.D. spoke slowly, as if trying to solve a complex puzzle.

"I always used to love that moment more than any other. Standing there at the top, full of possibilities, when nothing had gone wrong yet."

For a long moment, J.D. said nothing. As they passed one of the lift's support poles, they jounced around in their seats.

"Correct me if I'm wrong here—"

"Wouldn't be the first time."

"—but if you know you'll never have a kick-butt ride down the mountain again, it seems to me you've reached a certain level of resignation to your physical limitations."

"It sucks doesn't it?" Mitch missed the thrills of his old life. His feet dangled like lead weights off the chairlift, as if the ground already called to them to be firmly planted.

"But if you're resigned to being more careful, then doesn't that nullify your reasons for sending that leggy blond back to the Sunshine State?"

They started the long descent toward the ground, and surprisingly, Mitch didn't experience the dread he feared he might. Maybe this wouldn't be so bad, after all.

"How did you know why I sent her home?"

J.D. cast him a narrow look. "You don't know Ines very well, do you? I got a full report via cell phone on my way here today."

Mitch laughed. He wondered if Tessa had ripped him up one side and down the other when she related the story to her friend.

"But don't ignore the question. If you've come to terms with altering your lifestyle, why wouldn't you at least try a relationship with Tessa?"

Hadn't he asked himself that same question all night?

He gave J.D. the same answer he came up with time and time again. "But what if I screw up? What if I can't help but tempt fate and disappoint her? I've never been a model of self-restraint, you know. I'd not only let her down big-time, I'd break her heart."

"I can't believe it."

"What? That she cares about me that much?" Was it that hard to believe?

"That Mitch Ryder is running away from a challenge."

The quiet seemed endless. Only the frosty wind whistling past his ears disrupted the silence.

"You think I'm running away from Tessa?"

J.D. nodded with slow deliberation. "Never thought I'd see the day when you weren't up for a dare."

They reached the jumping-off point at the summit. J.D. grabbed his board while Mitch hopped off the lift.

Amazingly, Mitch didn't feel filled with angst to be on top of Whiteface. As he looked down the slope he knew so well, he couldn't conjure the regrets he'd thought would plague him.

Instead, he just felt good and mad that J.D. thought he was shirking a challenge. He glanced at his friend, who leaned over to tighten his boots and adjust his board.

"You know, I'm only doing what's best for her instead of thinking of myself for a change." Mitch turned away from the breathtaking mountain view to glare at J.D. "I'm surprised you don't see a little bit of nobility in that."

J.D. tugged his goggles over his eyes. "Nobility, eh? You can tell yourself that if it makes you feel better. But I think you're taking the safe way out because you're scared spitless that you'll screw up." He shrugged. "Of course, I've been wrong before."

Before Mitch could argue, J.D. crouched and leaned forward, pushing his snowboard into motion. He shouted over his shoulder. "See you at the bottom!"

Cold wind whistled in his wake.

Damn.

J.D. didn't know what he was talking about. Mitch had done the right thing to let Tessa go. Hadn't he?

He crunched through the packed snow at the top of

the mountain and started second-guessing himself. He hated thinking he might be running away.

But what if he took a gamble by marrying Tessa and then ended up succumbing to his adrenaline addiction anyway?

Pausing in mid-stride, Mitch faced the three thousand feet of vertical drop. Wind whipped around him. Blue sky enveloped him. The view stretched out for miles and gave Mitch the same impression it always had—that he stood on top of a world full of possibilities.

He sucked in the thin mountain air with deep breaths, recharged by the mood of the place.

He could stand here without longing to board down the mountain on one foot, couldn't he? He'd come here to face the mountain and ended up confronting a demon bigger than Whiteface. And damn it, he was winning.

Even as he encountered the temptation of a three-mile trail, he found himself thinking more about the thrills to be found in Tessa's bed than any excitement he might gain on the slopes. No way would he cave to the thrill-seeking fiend within if he married Tessa. He was stronger now than he had been eight years ago.

Now all he had to do was convince the boardroom barracuda.

If he wasn't too late.

"I'M GOING to be late." Tessa glanced at her watch for the third time in the last ten minutes. She stood beside Ines as her friend tried on her tenth wool headband in the Hearthside pro shop.

Ines glared at her. "I am hurrying as much I can,

chica. You know how I feel about accessorizing. These things take time."

"You can shop after I leave." Tessa retrieved her purse from the display table and tucked it under her arm. "I need to go."

"You would leave me to choose something un-chic just because you are in a hurry?" She looked as indignant as if Tessa had proposed they streak naked through the lobby.

"The ingrained teachings of a lifetime subscription to *Vogue* magazine ought to pull you through. I'm leaving."

Ines grumbled, but she gathered her other purchases and joined Tessa. "I do not know why you are in such a hurry to leave someone you are in lo—"

Tessa whirled to wave a finger in Ines's face. "Don't say it."

"But—"

"As far as I'm concerned, if no one admits those feelings, then they never really happened." She smiled tightly to cover the hurt inside her. She couldn't stand to hear the sad truth of her unreturned love spoken aloud. "Which, to my way of thinking, will make this whole matter easier to put behind me." Maybe if she kept lying to herself this way, she would start believing it one day.

Tessa stormed down the corridor, eager to get to her rental and get out of town.

"But if you wait a little longer, you might get to see Mitch before you—"

"The last person I want to see is Mitch!" Tessa hissed, barely controlling her temper. She really didn't want to fracture into a million pieces here. She wanted to wait until she was in the car and headed south.

"I'm sorry to hear that." The seductive baritone of Mitch intervened. "Because I really need to see you."

Oh, God.

Tessa heard herself gasp. She heard Ines utter a little happy squeal as if Mitch's appearance solved everything.

Ines darted away between the coat racks in a rustle of paper shopping bags, leaving Tessa and Mitch to talk alone.

Traitor.

"I—I really can't see you right now," Tessa murmured, shouldering her way past him in the hall.

"Wait." He stopped her with one hand to her shoulder.

Tessa recoiled. She definitely could not tolerate the bittersweet feel of his touch. Her brittle emotions would shatter like glass in an opera house.

"I mean, please wait."

She folded her arms and attempted to cut him down to size with a skeptical look she usually reserved for tense business negotiations. "What could you possibly have to say to me that you didn't already hammer home last night?"

"A few things, actually, if you'll just come sit with me for a minute."

There was no way on earth she was going to sit within ten feet of the walking aphrodisiac. She'd been sucked in by his charm one too many times to fall for that.

"No, thanks. I need to catch a plane." She launched

forward, determined to ignore him. "You can e-mail me if you need to reach me."

She marched toward the lobby, head held high despite her heavy heart. Behind her, Mitch's slightly uneven gait echoed in the hallway.

"Actually this is important enough that I think—"

"Is this in regard to Mogul Ryders?" She swung around to face him.

"No, but I—"

"Then, frankly, it's not that important." She resumed her trek, pausing at the courtesy desk to request that her luggage be sent out to her car. Then she turned to Mitch. "You crystallized everything for me yesterday. I definitely don't need to hear it again."

Plowing out the lobby's front doors, Tessa squinted into the bright sunlight. To a casual observer, she probably looked like a first-class shrew, stomping around the hotel as she tried to avoid him.

"Aren't you even a little curious about what I have to say?" If the rapid pounding of boots on wooden steps was any indication, Mitch sped down the front stairs behind her.

"No." She paused at the bottom of the steps. "Because even if you'd had a change of heart about us, or if you decided to give us another try, I would tell you that's a bad idea."

"Why?" His brow furrowed.

"Why? Because now I know how much of a strain a relationship would be for you if you constantly denied yourself the activities you love. I would never want you to do that for me."

And she wouldn't. Neither of them would be happy if Mitch always felt deprived of his thrills. He had been right last night to dispel any myths she held about a future together.

"I wouldn't be denying myself." He looked so sexy and solid and sure of himself. "I'm not drawn to that life anymore."

A quick thrill tripped through her until the doubt trickled in. Tessa wished she could believe him. She wanted nothing more than to wrap herself in those muscular arms and stay in Lake Placid forever. But to do that would kill Mitch's carefree spirit—one of the things that made him who he was.

Besides, trust didn't come easily to her after the way her husband had let her down.

She shook her head. "You were drawn to it yesterday, Mitch. People don't change overnight."

"I changed." He jerked a thumb in his own direction, his dark eyes glinting with a fierce light. "And it didn't happen overnight. It happened in a nanosecond of clear thinking."

"You don't need to—"

"Yes, I do. I need to explain to you what happened to me this morning so you understand how I can suddenly be so sure of what I want." He gripped her shoulders, physically drawing her into a conversation of which she wanted no part. "I faced the biggest temptation I know of today and walked away from it thinking how much more I care about you than any quest for a thrill."

"How can I trust that?" Tears clamored behind her eyes, but Tessa blinked fast to banish them before they fell. "I thought it hurt when my husband ran off with a skater and played me false, but I know it didn't come close to the hurt I'd feel if I lost you."

Mitch tugged her closer. "I'm telling you, I've put it behind me. Do you think I'm making this up?"

Tessa stood her ground, refusing to let his physical presence confuse her. "I think you're trying to make me happy at a terrible price to yourself, but it's not necessary." She took a deep breath to calm herself and prayed she would make it to her rental car before she fell apart. "Now, I really do have to leave."

As she turned away from Mitch and the Hearthside, a group of kids bundled in brightly colored Gore-Tex coats and wool scarves came charging down the cliffs behind the Hearthside. At first, she thought they were playing a loud game, but as the noisy troupe neared, she realized they were calling to her and Mitch.

"Help!" The two front runners in the pack of six children shouted and waved. Their eyes loomed wide with fright. "Please, help!"

Mitch gently squeezed Tessa's shoulders. "Don't go anywhere," he warned her before sprinting to meet the children at the bottom of the cliff.

She didn't know if she was grateful for the intrusion or upset. Somehow, she'd hoped in her heart Mitch would have found the words to convince her, a way to help her trust again.

She followed the group, hoping nothing was seriously wrong. And though she admired Mitch for rushing to the scared kids, she cringed to see him abuse his knee by running full speed to their aid. Her heart ached. Who would look out for him with her gone?

Nearing the assembled group, Tessa saw Mitch in the center of the pack, listening to the tallest boy.

"And then his board sorta slid out from under him.

And then he fell down the cliffs real far," the boy explained.

He couldn't have been more than eleven or twelve. His features were etched with fear, but he seemed to concentrate on getting his facts straight. "He made some weird noises, so I don't think he's dead or anything. But he looks awful hurt."

"Is anybody up there with him now?" Mitch asked.

The boy hovered on the verge of tears. "No, sir. We all came down to get help."

By now, a few other patrons from the hotel began to congregate around the scene. A woman beside Tessa pulled out a cell phone and called 911.

Mitch patted the tallest boy on the back. "It's okay, Brent. Go inside and find Joey's mom and tell her he fell. Tell her I'm going to go get him."

Oh, God.

Tessa envisioned Mitch paralyzed at the bottom of the treacherous cliffs. She'd never felt more wicked in her life than in that split second where she wished he wouldn't go.

But if a child was suffering down there, maybe even fatally injured, then someone had to help him.

Her gaze locked on Mitch. She knew he would risk himself for someone else. She only waited for him to say the inevitable.

Instead of running toward the cliffs, he bolted toward the hotel and shouted to her over his shoulder. "Get the snowboard off my truck. I'll be right back."

15

Mitch TOOK the hotel steps two at a time and prayed he wasn't making a mistake. While Daniela's son was stuck at the bottom of some of the most treacherous cliffs in town, Mitch ran for help like one of the kid's clueless ten-year-old friends.

But damn it, he couldn't afford to let the boy down with some misguided attempt to play hero and then end up falling butt over boots himself. With his bum knee, he very well could.

He couldn't risk both their necks when someone younger and more physically capable slept two flights away.

"Shawn!" Mitch pounded on his friend's door. "Get out here—"

The door flung wide to reveal Shawn in his boxer shorts. "You're gonna wake the whole damn hotel—"

"Joey fell down the cliffs doing some stunts on his board. You gotta go get him."

Shawn's first act was to pull on his pants. But as he scrambled around the room, searching for more clothes and boots, he pelted Mitch with questions.

"Is he okay?"

"I don't know. Someone called 911, but I know you could get down there quicker than any of the rescue people will be able to." Mitch found a boot under Shawn's bed. "Here's one."

"How will we get up there?" He shoved on his boot and grabbed a jacket as he headed for the door.

Mitch followed, filching a length of rope off Shawn's dresser on the way out. "The truck won't go through this snow. It'll be faster to run."

They sped out the door and down the wooden steps, their boots drumming the planks like a clogging team gone rogue.

Mitch saw Tessa in the hotel's backyard, wearing her trench coat and hugging his snowboard under one arm. For once, she'd had sense enough to wear boots. She gestured to someone in the parking lot when she spotted Mitch.

She hadn't suggested he shouldn't go down the cliffs to save Joey. He loved her for that, and for more things than he could count.

"Hurry!" she shouted to whoever she was waving to.

At her command, two snowmobiles roared to life. A man and a woman he didn't know pulled forward on the sleds and halted beside them. They hopped off, leaving the engines idling.

"Take these," Tessa shouted over the noise, handing Mitch the snowboard. "We'll be up with Daniela in a minute."

Out of the corner of his eye, he saw Joey's mother come out of the hotel with Ines. The poor woman looked terrified, but he knew his role wasn't to play comforter. Shawn would need his advice on the cliffs.

He and Shawn each took a snowmobile, leaving Tessa to round up more snowmobiles and coordinate the rest of the rescue effort. If he hadn't been scared to death that Joey might be hurt, he would have smiled at the notion of his boardroom barracuda taking charge.

They reached the cliff's edge and killed the engines. The sudden stillness, the silence, seemed more ominous than their frenzied efforts to get there.

"Joey!" Mitch shouted over the edge, searching the landscape one hundred yards below. The ground dropped off at about a sixty-degree angle, making the slope treacherous but not unnavigable.

He didn't hear any response, but Shawn jabbed him in the arm.

"There's a patch of color over there." Shawn pointed northward, to a spot of neon lime almost hidden among the evergreens.

"Joey!" Mitch shouted again.

No answer.

"What do I do?" Shawn looked worried and not a minute older than his twenty-one years.

"I can still go," Mitch assured him, hating to think he'd pressured his friend into this. "You know I can do this. But I have faith that you can, too, or I wouldn't have asked you."

The fear vanished from Shawn's eyes. "Yeah. If you didn't get lost on the way down, old man." He pulled on his goggles and grabbed Mitch's board. "I could read these slopes in my sleep, too. But why don't you give me your take on it, just for the hell of it."

"Start here." Mitch's heart pumped the worst kind of adrenaline through his system. He wasn't worried about Shawn any longer. The kid could get down there okay. But the thought of Joey alone and hurt put a terrible price tag on failure.

Shutting that notion out of his mind, he stood with

Shawn at the edge of the cliffs and pointed out the best trail down the perilous terrain.

BY THE TIME Tessa had found a snowmobile for Daniela and Ines, then directed the fire rescue crew to the accident scene, fifteen minutes had passed.

She knew because she checked her watch every ten seconds and wondered if Mitch was okay.

At least he'd had sense enough to bring Shawn with him. That way there would be someone to get more help if the legendary Mogul Ryder lost control on his course down the incline.

She'd been shocked and relived that he'd taken the time to retrieve his friend before undertaking a dangerous task. The old Mitch would have leaped right in without a thought for his safety. But that small amount of caution wasn't enough to convince her he'd left his thrill-seeking days behind him.

The fact that he had rushed to the boy's rescue, even though Lake Placid was full of world champions in every facet of downhill sports, proved as much. Earlier, he'd tried to tell her didn't need that kind of life anymore, that he didn't have to conquer all of life's challenges, but he'd contradicted his own words an hour later.

Not that she blamed him. For once, his hunger for a challenge could be put to good use if he could save a child's life.

J.D. pulled into the parking lot just as she started to wonder how she would get to the cliffs now that she'd directed everyone else up there.

"What's going on?" he shouted, getting out of his car among fire trucks and an EMS van.

"A local boy fell down the cliffs, and Mitch went to help get him out." She had one last snowmobile earmarked for her use. "You want to head up there with me?"

At his nod, they hopped on the machine and traversed the snow between the hotel and the cliff. Tessa filled him in on what few details she knew. When they neared the top of the bluff and killed the engine, a small knot of onlookers parted for them, allowing her and J.D. to see the edge of the cliff drop off into the horizon.

And there was Mitch.

Lying on his stomach, firmly planted on the upper terrain, he spoke into a two-way radio. Someone had provided him with a pair of binoculars, and he peered through them while he gave instructions into the receiver.

"Veer left just a little." He sounded as calm as if he was reeling off the benefits of his new line of snowboards, while everyone around him wore expressions ranging from anxious to somber. "You need to pick up speed, Shawn. There's a jump in maybe twenty feet."

Tessa couldn't believe it. Mitch had stepped out of the limelight, ignored a big challenge and let Shawn go down the cliffs on his own.

After a minute of utter silence, Mitch pumped his fist in the air and the members of the fire rescue squad let out a whoop.

"He's got him!" Mitch turned as he shouted the news. "He did it."

He sounded like a proud father. Or coach. It occurred to her that he would be great in either role.

Their eyes locked for a moment. The jolt of desire

that had always plagued her when he was around sizzled with hot insistence. She'd never wanted him—or
loved him—so much.

"How is my baby?" Daniela's voice, still choked
with fear, rose above the low noise of the crowd.

Tessa pulled her gaze from Mitch to see the boy's
mother. She was flanked by Ines and J.D., her face
creased with worry, her cheeks stained with tears and
forgotten mascara.

Mitch passed the two-way radio to Daniela. "He
wants to speak to you."

The maid rushed forward, oblivious to the snow
around her stockinged ankles. "Thank God."

Tessa stared at her openly, along with the fifty other
people who'd gathered around. Relief flooded her
when Daniela smiled.

"He says he's just having a bad day," Daniela called
to the crowd. The glow of maternal love transcended
the woman's smeared makeup and disheveled hair,
rimming her with a beauty that brought tears to
Tessa's eyes.

Mitch snagged her glance and took a step toward
her, but the fire rescue chief intercepted him. Tessa
moved closer, needing to feel Mitch's strength and vitality after the panicked hour she'd spent fearing for
his life.

As if sensing her wish, he reached out to her even as
the rescue official commanded his attention. He
tucked her under one arm and kissed the top of her
head.

The tall, middle-aged woman who wore the chief's
hat lowered her voice to speak to Mitch, cognizant of
the throng of onlookers. "How serious did it sound?"

Mitch shrugged. "Sounded to me like maybe he has a broken leg. Shawn says it looks twisted."

In the background of Mitch's quiet words, Tessa could hear the tearful encouragement Daniela administered to her son over the radio. "Shawn will get you out of there, sweetheart. Listen to what he says. You'll feel better once you can see a doctor."

The EMS people tossed a medical kit down the cliffs while the chief continued to speak with Mitch.

"I would recommend that your friend haul him out on the snowboard, sort of sled style. It will help keep the leg immobilized. Is there a way we can access the bottom of these cliffs so the boy can be pulled downward instead of trying to drag him upward?"

"They empty out just above the new Two Chimneys Inn. I think if you take the access road to the kitchen it would put you right about where you need to be."

The chief nodded, then turned to shout directions to her squad. Tessa watched the woman commandeer the radio from Daniela and inform Shawn of the latest plan to move Joey to safety.

Tessa looked at Mitch, yearning to reconnect with him, hoping she hadn't lost her opportunity to salvage things with him this morning. "You think it will work to pull the boy out on the snowboard?"

Together, they watched the rescue trucks load up for relocation. Other members of the crowd started down the hill toward the Hearthside.

He nodded. "The hard part was getting there. We wanted to get down the cliffs in a hurry in case Joey was seriously hurt. But now that we know he's breathing okay, we've got more time on our side.

Shawn can pull him out if he zigzags across the slopes."

Reassured, Tessa leaned into him, savoring the solid feel of him. This was a man she could trust, a man who could give her a relationship with roots no matter how far they traveled. "Thank you for letting Shawn go in your place."

"He's determined to take my place in every way he can." A rueful grin tugged at his lips.

Tessa ran leather-covered fingers across his square jaw. "I know one particular arena in which he'll never claim your place, handsome."

He pulled her closer and grazed his mouth over hers in a kiss that left her breathless and hopeful.

"Would you be making sweet promises like that if I hadn't played such a reserved role in Joey's rescue today?" His gaze pinned her, forcing her to confront her feelings for him.

"Maybe not." She wouldn't lie to him. She wouldn't run away from her feelings for him anymore. The time had come to trust, to let down the barriers that had protected her since her husband walked away from her. "Your willingness to stand on the sidelines made me realize you truly have left your reckless days behind. But I'd like to think you'd have found another way to make me listen sooner or later."

He smoothed his hands down the shoulders of her trench coat. She shivered, dreaming about the moment he would take it off of her later, when they were alone.

"Thank God I didn't have to slog it out for a year as a librarian to get you to take me seriously."

She studied the hard planes of his face, the heavy-lidded eyes that had always set her pulse racing. "I don't know. You would look very drool-worthy in a pair of those little banker's glasses, you know. The librarian look might have really suited you."

"Yeah? I think I sense a snowball fight coming on." He shook his finger at her. "You might want to get a head start down the hill."

Tessa spied the snowmobiles Mitch and Shawn had ridden and smiled. "I'm taking a snowmobile, and you'll be eating exhaust fumes."

He looped his arms around her neck to halt her. "You won't be going anywhere, honey. I'm not letting you get away from me for a second time."

"Promise?" His words brought joy to her heart. A vision of herself ensconced in a snowbound cabin, tapping away at her computer while she sat near an aromatic fire, filled her with contentment.

He cradled her face in his hands. "Promise. And I'm backing it up with at least a full carat."

"You don't need to back it up with anything more than a kiss." She couldn't wait to get him alone, to lock herself in his bedroom and hold him captive for days to fulfill every fantasy she'd had about him over the last eight years. "But if that was a proposal, Mitch Ryder, my answer is yes."

He squeezed her to him and laughed. "Honey, you sure know how to close a deal. They don't call you the boardroom barracuda for nothing."

"No one calls me that." She frowned. "The bedroom bombshell, maybe." She walked her fingers up his chest. "Or board-selling babe..."

He groaned. "Stop it, woman. You're making me want you too much."

She pulled away, feeling sexy and loved and more full of herself than she had in a long time. Marrying Mitch was going to be a very, very good thing.

"Then let's see how fast we can get to the bottom of these cliffs and make sure Shawn pulls Joey down successfully." She tugged him toward the snowmobiles. "We can't indulge ourselves until we make sure everyone gets out of this safely."

Mitch nodded. "I wouldn't want to miss Shawn's next triumph."

She smiled, realizing that he really cared about Shawn, no matter how much he joked about him.

"Besides," Mitch added, scratching his jaw. "I think we should make sure the Mogul Ryder board gets in the newspaper photos along with him. Don't you?"

"You're too much." She laughed as she turned the key that brought the snowmobile to life. "What did you ever need marketing help for, anyway?"

Mitch surprised her by straddling the machine behind her. They wouldn't get to the bottom quite as fast this way, but the ride would sure be more fun. His thighs bracketed hers, sending a rush of heat through her limbs that had nothing to do with the purring motor beneath them.

He leaned close to whisper in her ear over the rev of the engine. His voice tantalized her senses like fingernails on a lover's back. "Maybe I was just in the market for you."

Receive 2 FREE Trade books with 4 proofs
of purchase from Harlequin Temptation® books.

HARLEQUIN®

Temptation.

You will receive:

Dangerous Desires: Three complete novels by
Jayne Ann Krentz, Barbara Delinsky and Anne Stuart

and

Legacies of Love: Three complete novels by
Jayne Ann Krentz, Stella Cameron and Heather Graham

Simply complete the order form and mail to:
"Temptation 2 Free Trades Offer"

In U.S.A.	In CANADA
P.O. Box 9057	P.O. Box 622
3010 Walden Avenue	Fort Erie, Ontario
Buffalo, NY 14269-9057	L2A 5X3

YES! Please send me *Dangerous Desires* and *Legacies of Love*, without
cost or obligation except shipping and handling. Enclosed are 4 proofs
of purchase from September or October 2002 Harlequin Temptation
books and $3.75 shipping and handling fees. New York State residents
must add applicable sales tax to shipping and handling charge.
Canadian residents must add 7% GST to shipping and handling charge.

Name (PLEASE PRINT)

Address   Apt. #

City   State/Prov.   Zip/Postal Code

TEMPTATION 2 FREE TRADES OFFER TERMS
To receive your FREE trade books, please complete the above
form. Mail it to us with 4 proofs of purchase, one of which can
be found in the lower right-hand corner of this page. Requests
must be received no later than November 30, 2002. Please
include $3.75 for shipping and handling fees and applicable
taxes as stated above. The 2 FREE Trade books are valued at
$12.95 U.S./$14.95 CAN. each. All orders are subject to
approval. Terms and prices are subject to change without
notice. Please allow 6-8 weeks for delivery. Offer good in
Canada and the U.S. only. Offer good while quantities last.
Offer limited to one per household.

Temptation.
2 FREE TRADES OFFER
One Proof of Purchase

HARLEQUIN®
Makes any time special ®

HTPOPFT

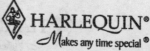

Princes...Princesses...
London Castles...New York Mansions...
To live the life of a royal!

In 2002, Harlequin Books lets you escape to a
world of royalty with these royally themed titles:

Temptation:
January 2002—*A Prince of a Guy* (#861)
February 2002—*A Noble Pursuit* (#865)

American Romance:
The Carradignes: American Royalty (Editorially linked series)
March 2002—*The Improperly Pregnant Princess* (#913)
April 2002—*The Unlawfully Wedded Princess* (#917)
May 2002—*The Simply Scandalous Princess* (#921)
November 2002—*The Inconveniently Engaged Prince* (#945)

Intrigue:
The Carradignes: A Royal Mystery (Editorially linked series)
June 2002—*The Duke's Covert Mission* (#666)

Chicago Confidential
September 2002—*Prince Under Cover* (#678)

The Crown Affair
October 2002—*Royal Target* (#682)
November 2002—*Royal Ransom* (#686)
December 2002—*Royal Pursuit* (#690)

Harlequin Romance:
June 2002—*His Majesty's Marriage* (#3703)
July 2002—*The Prince's Proposal* (#3709)

Harlequin Presents:
August 2002—*Society Weddings* (#2268)
September 2002—*The Prince's Pleasure* (#2274)

Duets:
September 2002—*Once Upon a Tiara/Henry Ever After* (#83)
October 2002—*Natalia's Story/Andrea's Story* (#85)

Celebrate a year of royalty with
Harlequin Books!
Available at your favorite retail outlet.

HARLEQUIN®
Makes any time special ®
Visit us at www.eHarlequin.com

HSROY02

The holidays have descended on

COOPER'S CORNER

providing a touch of seasonal magic!

Coming in November 2002...
MY CHRISTMAS COWBOY
by Kate Hoffmann

Check-in: Bah humbug! That's what single mom
Grace Penrose felt about Christmas this year. All her plans
for the Cooper's Corner Christmas Festival are going wrong—
and now she finds out she has an unexpected houseguest!

Checkout: But sexy cowboy Tucker McCabe is no ordinary
houseguest, and Grace feels her spirits start to lift. Suddenly
she has the craziest urge to stand under the mistletoe...forever!

HARLEQUIN®
Makes any time special ®

Visit us at www.cooperscorner.com

CC-CNM4